Wild

Roses, Volume 1

Lucy Winton

Cover designed with BookBrush Cover Creator

ISBN: 9781686614125

For my mother. Without her, this series wouldn't
have been possible.

Want a free novella?

Visit my website at:
https://www.lucywintonauthor.com/

Prologue

It was the last sunrise she'd ever see at Kindainn. If Milly kept her eyes on the sky she'd be less tempted to look at the houses behind them and she *wasn't* going to look back.

She'd known this day was coming. Now it was here, it didn't quite seem real.

"Are you cold, Milly?" her mother asked.

"A little bit. But I'm OK."

It probably wasn't going to get any warmer. The clouds in the sky looked as if they were only going to get heavier. Milly was grateful it wasn't windy or raining.

"I hope they don't keep us waiting for long," her father muttered.

"They won't," Milly's mother replied. Her hair was tied away from her face, just like her daughter's. Out of the three Costello sisters, Milly was the one who'd inherited their mother's blonde hair, pale blue eyes and slight figure. "The letter said to be out here promptly, and we are. They're not going to..."

Milly was only half-listening. She preferred to concentrate instead on the sounds of the nearest river trickling past them and the birdsong. Grant would be getting up now to start the day; if she inhaled hard enough, she thought she could catch the scent of baking. Everyone in Kindainn ate warm, fresh bread each morning. Why hadn't Milly ever appreciated that?

Her throat felt as if a cord was slowly tightening around it, but she refused to cry.

The birdsong changed sharply. Two figures strode towards them over the open field. Milly's mouth suddenly went dry. She clutched both straps of her knapsack so that her hands wouldn't start shaking.

There were only two kinds of Wolf-Lord in the stories Milly had heard. The first was lean and powerful, with half-starved beasts crouching at their sides. The second was ruthless, ordering their wolves to tear out their enemies' throats. Artists always drew those wolves crouching over the corpses, teeth bared in a snarl, blood dripping from their jaws.

"You're the Costellos?" the approaching Wolf-Lord demanded as soon as she reached them. "You're Craig, Teresa and Emilia?" She had shoulder-length brown hair that she'd obviously cut herself and was wearing a green, dirt-stained jacket, faded jeans and black boots. Milly's eyes strayed briefly towards the large brown wolf beside her before quickly returning to the woman's face and the black scarf tied around her neck.

"That's us," Milly's father replied. They were the only family in Kindainn to reply to Premier Barton's letter.

"I'm Gabrielle Weatherhill." Weatherhill's eyes roamed over Milly's face. "How old is she?"

"I'm fifteen," Milly said. A cold breeze blew across the river and she suppressed a shiver. The Premier made it clear nobody under the age of thirteen could join the migration.

The wolf nudged impatiently at Weatherhill's leg, growling softly. Its eyes seemed to glint in the early morning light. "All right," she said, scratching the back of its neck briefly. "Follow me and we'll join the others."

As they walked away, Milly forced herself to keep looking ahead. They hadn't been able to take anything with them except some clothes, shoes and a few tiny trinkets able to fit into their bags. Barton assured them everything they would need would be provided for them in Redcross: a new house, new furniture, new friends, and new jobs. A new life.

The Costellos had said their farewells the day before. Just as Milly was saying goodbye to Louise, their neighbour, the old woman took hold of her wrist; her touch was light and dry as paper, but it held Milly still.

"Do not act fearful around Wolf-Lords or their beasts," she whispered. "If you do, they will think you are prey."

The words hadn't sunk in then.

"Let me give you a word of advice now," Weatherhill said without looking at any of the Costellos. "Don't lag behind. Premier Barton said to get all of you to Redcross safely, but I won't put up with stragglers."

The wolf growled again. This time, there was a definite note of warning.

"We understand," Milly's father said. He put a hand on Milly's shoulder and squeezed; Milly couldn't tell if it was meant to be reassuring or another warning.

Her pink dress lay nestled at the very bottom of her knapsack. It was the first thing she'd thought to pack, probably the last piece of clothing she'd need and the one thing she couldn't imagine leaving behind.

The sun peered through the clouds, ready to warm the earth below.

Chapter 1

Two Years Later

Milly was unable to see much of the sky through the glass door because of the buildings blocking her view, but she could see crimson fading to mauve, with dark purple clouds slowly drifting across it. She wondered if her eldest sister was looking at a similar sunset right now, or if Rachel was too busy painting something else.

"Milly!" Carlene called. "The announcement's almost on!"

"I'm just coming!" Milly dropped the cloth she was holding onto the nearest table and hurried over to where Sami, Avrel and Carlene were clustered around the small screen.

"Can I turn up the volume?" Avrel asked, turning to look at Carlene. Her brown hair, so carefully tied on top of her head in the morning, now hung around her face in untidy tendrils.

"Go on," was the reply.

"I don't understand," said Sami. "Why is this announcement so important?" Unlike the others, she sat delicately on the edge of the nearest table. Since Layden's Café didn't have any customers, Carlene didn't tell her to get down.

"Let's find out." Milly folded her arms and watched Roy Barton's face appear on the screen. Avrel pressed the volume buttons as the Premier started speaking.

"It's recently come to my attention that the safety measures I implemented are not as effective as they should be."

"It only took him two years to notice," Sami murmured.

"Shh!" Carlene's eyes darted to the open door, but nobody had walked into Layden's while she and the girls were focusing on the screen.

"My head of security, Captain Trevel, will be taking some time away from Redcross. Her replacement will arrive..."

"Do you think 'taking some time away' is a nice way of saying 'being put on probation'?" asked Avrel, fiddling with one of the woven bracelets around her wrists.

"I don't know, but look, he's still talking." Milly pointed at Barton, who was still addressing the cameras and the people assembled in the Complex.

"...and I have made a deal with the Andras Wolf-Lords in order to ensure the security of Redcross." He spoke over the shocked murmurs and gasps to announce: "They will be arriving in the city tomorrow and I expect everyone here to greet them warmly."

"Their wolves will probably kill us if we don't," Avrel muttered.

Sami shuddered, clutching the edge of the table. "Please don't make jokes like that."

"Did I sound like I was joking?"

There were rumours of Wolf-Lords encouraging their wolves to tear a person to shreds as quickly and easily as they would a deer. The girls knew wolves were naturally capable of that. The mere notion of killing one person at the command of another was terrifying. It wasn't true of every Wolf-Lord, but the rumours made people treat them with fear more than with respect.

Frankie came out of the kitchen, drying her hands on a towel. Her hazel eyes darted to the screen. "What have I missed?"

Avrel laughed, shaking her head incredulously. "Only you would miss something like that, Frankie."

"Just tell me what's happened! It's got to be important, you wouldn't have put the sound on if it wasn't." Frankie put the towel down on the nearest table.

"We had the sound on and you still didn't hear it?" Sami asked.

"The kitchen door was shut, and you didn't have the sound at full volume."

"Never mind. The Premier's just announced a deal with the Andras Wolf-Lords," Carlene said matter-of-factly.

"He's *what?*" Frankie looked from Carlene to her friends in complete shock. "You're not serious."

"They'll be here tomorrow," Avrel told her.

"Wait, the *Andras* Wolf-Lords? Where do they come from?" Frankie asked. "I've never heard of them."

"I've no idea." Sami shrugged delicately. "Maybe they're a new group - or maybe it's an old group with a new leader. The name changes when there's a new leader."

"You should be all right with them, shouldn't you?" asked Carlene, picking up the towel Frankie had used. She wrinkled her nose at its tattered state and scrunched it into a ball. "Wolf-Lords escorted you to Redcross in the first place; I bet you're used to being around wolves."

Milly turned away from the screen and walked over to the cutlery drawer. The nearest table needed two more knives and forks. She selected the right utensils and put them at the right places on the table, with a folded napkin to the right of the knife. "It's going to be strange having them in the city. It'll probably be even stranger for them."

The truth was, she didn't think she had grown used to the wolves. She and everyone else on the journey simply tried their best to ignore them as much as possible.

For a moment, she felt a little envious of the Wolf-Lords. She knew she and her friends didn't have a bad deal when it came to Layden's Café. In fact, Milly realised after her first ten days that it was a good arrangement. Avrel, Milly, Frankie and Sami cooked, washed up and served at the tables and in exchange, ate lunch and supper there for free.

But Milly remembered the world outside Redcross. She'd lived in it, travelled through it. She still dreamed about rivers running through the woods, vast open fields and sky above.

She was not going to spend the rest of her life inside the city's walls.

Carlene clapped her hands together. "Since we don't have any customers, let's talk about food. We've got a lot of potatoes in the store, so we'll do potato soup tomorrow with tomato sandwiches. Milly, could you do something with the apples before they go rotten?"

"What about a cake? I think we've still got some cinnamon left."

"All right, but don't use too much. Sami, I need you to go to the market tomorrow and get some tomatoes, mushrooms and whatever fruit is on offer. Oh, and see if there's any good fish. We're all right for flour, milk and cheese for the next few days."

"Do we have enough eggs?" asked Avrel.

"Good point. I'll have a look. Now, we've got a couple of slices of pie, some sausages from breakfast and some soup, but there's only enough soup for two of us. It was very popular today."

"I'll have some!" Frankie cried. "Anyone else?"

Milly, Sami and Avrel looked at each other. Eventually, Avrel shrugged and raised a hand.

"I'll warm it up," she said. "How long before the drums?"

Carlene looked at the clock anxiously. "Not that long, so we'd better eat quickly. That announcement took longer than I thought."

The door opened, sending a jingling sound through the café. Everyone suppressed a groan and turned instinctively with welcoming smiles on their faces...only for the smiles to disappear when they saw a young man with dark blond hair in the doorway.

"Uh-oh," Frankie muttered.

"Hey, Carlene," the newcomer said, his cheeks dimpling as they always did when he smiled.

"A little late to be out, isn't it, Jason?" asked Carlene. "And don't tell me you're just dropping by. You never do that."

"Really? I don't?"

"No, you don't," Sami said, folding her arms. "What are you doing here?" A wisp of black hair managed to escape her ponytail; she delicately brushed it behind her ear.

Jason's smile quailed a little as his eyes fell on Avrel. "I just came here to..." He scratched above his left ear with one hand. "Hey, um, Avrel, when you see Leo, could you tell him I said thanks?"

"It'll be hard to tell him with a guard there," Avrel replied coolly. "Leo hasn't earned the privilege of unsupervised visits yet."

"Oh. Right. Well, just tell him I said hi." With one final grin, Jason backed out of the café.

Avrel whirled around and went into the kitchen. Nobody went after her.

Once she emerged, two bowls of warm soup in her hands, Frankie said: "I guess there's no point in asking if you're still angry with him."

13

Avrel set the bowls down on the nearest table. She didn't answer. Frankie took the opportunity and slipped past her into the kitchen to get the rest of the food.

"What are you upset about?" asked Carlene. "Is it that Jason got Leo into running, or that Leo was arrested while Jason wasn't? Leo knew what he was getting into. Nobody forced him to do it."

"I know. That's the worst part." Avrel pushed herself into a chair and picked up her spoon.

Frankie reappeared with the sausages and pie. "Shall we just change the subject?"

Avrel dug her spoon into the soup. "Let's do that. I hate eating in awkward silence."

"So tell me about the Wolf-Lords," Carlene said. "What are they actually like?"

The girls looked at each other.

"Tell me," prompted Carlene. "I'm fascinated. Are the stories actually true?"

"Which stories?" asked Milly. She had no idea which of the myths and legends about the Wolf-Lords were real and which were not, and she hadn't dared to approach one of their chaperones to ask them.

Nobody doubted the tales originating from the wars were true.

"Any of them. All of them."

"Weatherhill's wolf was the leader." Sami poured Frankie another glass of water. "The Wolf-Lords answered to Weatherhill, the wolves answered to her wolf and to their humans, and Weatherhill and her wolf answered to each other. It's a dual leadership."

There was a sharp rattling sound in the distance that slowly grew louder. Milly turned to see a figure in a dark uniform walking past the café door, beating repetitively on a small drum. She could just about see people scurrying away in the dim light.

Carlene sighed and put her fork down. "Don't worry about clearing up. I'll take care of it."

Milly and the girls hurried outside the café. The echoes of the drumbeats still hung in the air.

"I'll see you tomorrow," Milly said before trotting down the street. Her friends were all going in the opposite direction, and there was no need or time for a long goodbye. Not after the drums sounded.

Curfew would start soon, and nobody wanted to be arrested by the Watchmen.

The lamps flickered on, lighting the streets with a pale orange glow. Milly took care to stay out of the shadows, avoiding people rushing past her on their way home. She was glad she'd thought to put her fleece on before the announcement started, otherwise she might have forgotten it.

When she and her family first arrived, she needed somebody to escort her home a few times so that she wouldn't get lost. Watchmen did not take 'being lost' as an excuse to be out after curfew.

Now she knew the route so well, she could have walked it without the lamps.

***

Nobody locked their doors in Redcross. The downstairs lights in Milly's house were on, which meant at least one of her parents was home. She pushed open the door.

"Hi, I'm back!"

"Hi, darling!" her mother called from the kitchen. "Did you get much to eat?"

A couple of sandwiches for lunch and a single slice of pie for dinner wasn't what Teresa Costello would have considered a proper meal back in Kindainn. But things were different now and Milly's mother only had to prepare food for two. "I did, thanks, Mum."

"Are you sure? We've got some scrambled eggs left over."

"Does that mean you prepared too much, or you deliberately left some?" Milly got her answer when she walked into the kitchen and saw a small plate of eggs on the counter. It was one of the few plates her parents didn't use. She sighed. *"Mum."*

"I know you're working now, but I'm your mother and it's still my job to look after you."

"My friends won't have food waiting for them."

"Then it's a good thing you're my daughter."

There was no point in arguing further, so Milly

15

reluctantly began to eat the eggs. They were still warm.

"Have *you* had enough to eat?" she asked.

"Yes, we have." Her mother's tone said the matter wasn't to be discussed further. She waited until the plate was empty before holding out a sheet of paper. "Oh, by the way, a messenger delivered this earlier."

"Is it from Susanna?" Milly asked eagerly. "Yes. Do you want to read it now?"

Milly hesitated. "Is it OK if I read it in private?"

"Yes, as long as you give it to your father so that he can..."

Teresa blanched. "Your father. He's not back." She looked at her watch. "It's only seven minutes until curfew starts."

"What? But you've cooked dinner; why did he go back out again?"

"He wanted to talk to Mr White about our broken table, so he went next door." Mr White was a joiner who did carpentry jobs when his services weren't needed by Premier Barton and other high-ranking members of Redcross.

"Do we have enough to pay him?"

"We should. If we don't, we can live without a table for a bit."

The front door opened and shut again. "Hello!" Mother and daughter relaxed as Craig walked into the kitchen.

"Hi, Dad." Milly carried her plate over to the sink and ran cold water over it.

"Sorry I'm back so late. The Whites wouldn't have liked it if I'd had to stay until curfew was over." Craig's eyes fell on the letter in his wife's hand, then his gaze drifted over to his daughter. "Go on and read it, Milly. I'm happy to wait."

Milly grinned, snatched the message and scampered upstairs to her bedroom. She closed the door, sat down on her bed and began to greedily read her sister's words.

Hi everyone,

I hope you're all well. If Rachel gets in touch with you, please give her my love.

I'm sorry this letter's so short, but the truth is not

much has been happening. I've been very tired lately because a lot of my research involves staying up late and reading. It's strange - I used to read late at night because I wanted to, and now I'm doing it because I have to.

Edwin's been keeping me company in the library, and I'm so grateful! It's always better to study with someone else, especially when the library is so quiet.

I can't believe I'm halfway through my studies here. Every time I think I've learned something new, I find out so much more. I miss your cooking, Mum. The food at the Academy just isn't up to your standard.

Please write to me soon.

Lots of love, Susanna

Milly folded up the letter. "I miss you too, Susy."

Chapter 2

Two Years Ago

"All right!" Weatherhill shouted. "We eat, rest for two hours, and then we move on."

Milly shrugged off her knapsack and sat down beside the nearest tree, leaning back against its trunk. The bark was rough on the back of her head.

Weatherhill had led them to a large clearing filled with fallen trees. Hardly anyone spoke while walking; now, soft laughter and talk wafted through the air.

Milly tensed as padding feet drew closer. A gangly wolf walked up and stood in front of her. Milly's hands tightened around a tree root. She knew if she made eye contact the wolf would see it as a challenge, but she couldn't look away. She couldn't move. She couldn't even blink.

"Aela!"

The wolf's ears twitched, and she stepped away towards a young black-haired Wolf-Lord. Milly closed her eyes and breathed out slowly, relief flooding her limbs.

Now the wolf was gone, Milly had to admit she was a beautiful creature: black fur tipped with grey, with lighter fur around her chest and muzzle.

"Are you all right?"

Milly looked up at her mother and nodded. "I'm fine, Mum."

"Good. Just...try not to provoke them. I'm sure that's not what you were doing, but please be careful."

Lunch was white dumplings cooked in water from the river, strips of dried salted meat and dried fruit. Even while sitting, Weatherhill was never at rest. Her eyes darted everywhere, following every noise she heard, all the while never meeting anyone's gaze.

Milly ate slowly, gazing around at the other travellers. Most sat in small groups; others ate by themselves, not seeming to want to speak to anyone. She wondered if they'd left an open town like Kindainn or a walled city like Redcross, and whether the people eating together had come from the same place. A lot looked like they were in their twenties or early thirties, but Milly had never been good at telling a person's age.

How many people were in the other groups travelling to Redcross? To her disappointment, there didn't seem to be anyone her age in this one.

Wait - there was someone. A girl sat on a fallen tree, twirling a strand of her long black hair around one finger, a discarded bowl by her feet. Even though she was wearing a green fleece, dark trousers and black boots, she looked like a forest nymph.

Milly's beaker still had a little water in it. She got up and walked over to the girl, clutching her beaker tightly.

"Hi," she said. "I'm Milly."

The girl looked up at her with a lazy curiosity. Her eyes were the colour of sun-kissed leaves and her pale skin looked as delicate as silk.

"I'm Samara. Where are you from? I'm sorry," she said before Milly could reply. "A lot of people are going to ask where you're from. I find it really irritating."

She edged to one side, giving Milly room to sit beside her. Her family was - or had been - rich; her clothes, although flecked with dirt, looked as though they were made of finer material than the other travellers' clothes were.

"Welcome to the journey," Samara said, raising her beaker. Milly touched her beaker to Samara's in a gesture she'd seen her parents do many times.

***

Now

"Do you miss Kindainn?" Milly asked suddenly.

Her mother looked at her in surprise. "Yes, Milly. Why do you ask?"

Milly shook her head. "Nothing; I just wondered, that's all."

Teresa slid a bowl of porridge and a small cup across the side to her daughter. "Hope the tea's not too strong. Some mornings, I open my eyes and I'm still surprised to find myself in Redcross. Truth is, I think I knew we wouldn't be in Kindainn for long after Rachel left and when Susanna said she wanted to apply to the Academy, it was just a matter of time."

Premier Barton's letter must have seemed like the perfect chance.

"But yes, I miss it," Teresa mused softly. "I grew up there, just like you did, but it was time to move on. Your sisters had a fresh start and we hoped we'd get the same for you. Let's be honest, there wasn't anything for you back in Kindainn."

Milly hadn't thought of it like that. She'd never known her parents had ambitions for her. An image of Kindainn flashed in her mind: rivers safe enough to swim in, blossom on the trees, carefully tended rose bushes planted alongside the paths and around the small houses.

If it was a choice between that and Redcross, she knew which one she'd take. Yet if they hadn't left, she wouldn't have met the girls, and she was so glad she had.

"We just thought you'd find something better here."

Milly steeled herself against the regret in her mother's voice and swallowed a spoonful of porridge. There was a small drizzle of golden honey on the top. "This is perfect. Thanks, Mum."

Milly's father chose that moment to walk in. "Zach said the table will be finished by tonight; he's coming over to pick it up later. Ready for another day of kitchen slavery, Milly?"

"Almost." The tea was far too hot to gulp down quickly. Milly winced as the liquid went down her throat, not quite sure if her father was joking or not.

She hoped there was cake left over today.

After finishing the porridge, she picked up her fleece from the nearest chair. "Bye! See you later."

With her parents' goodbyes following her, she left the house and went on her way to Layden's.

The Costello family lived on a quiet street with no gardens. There hadn't been nearly enough emigrants to fill all the unoccupied houses in Redcross; many of the buildings would always have darkened windows unless others arrived to fill them. The Costello house wasn't on the outskirts of the city, so it wasn't long before houses were replaced with empty shops and other businesses. The booktrader was unlocking his door; he nodded to Milly before stepping inside and closing the door behind him.

Milly wondered if Sami would get a chance to visit the booktrader soon. She was choosy about the books she read but every time she picked one, she would read it over and over until it sank into her mind.

The library in the correction facility probably held older and far more interesting books than the booktrader could ever hope to get his hands on.

Avrel and Sami were already outside Layden's. Sami leaned against the wall, her eyes raised to the sky while Avrel paced in front of the door. This time, she'd used her favourite scarf to tie her hair back and away from her forehead. Even though Sami only wore a simple pair of jeans, her green fleece and a purple T-shirt that went perfectly with her hair, she managed to make them look classy and ladylike.

Milly went up to them. "Hi," she said. "Hasn't she unlocked the door yet?"

Carlene always had Layden's door unlocked before the girls arrived so that they could start cooking breakfast using the ingredients waiting for them in the kitchen.

The first customers would arrive soon.

"Not yet." Avrel stopped pacing and peered through the glass door, trying to catch a glimpse of Carlene in the café's murky insides.

Frankie came racing down the street and skidded to a halt, barely avoiding a collision with Milly. "I am so sorry I'm late," she panted. She looked at the others in confusion. "What are we doing standing outside?"

"I don't know." Milly put her hand on the glass door. It was cold under her palm. "I hope Carlene's all right." Out of the corner of her eye, she saw Sami and Avrel glance worriedly at each other; it might not have occurred to them that Carlene's absence wasn't voluntary.

There was movement in the shadows. All four girls sighed audibly as Carlene emerged from her home above Layden's and switched on the light in the main part of the café. She smiled and waved to the girls.

"Sorry about that," she said as she opened the door to let them in. "I lost something, and it was pretty hard to find."

Milly's eyes fell on Carlene's left hand, where she always wore two wedding rings: her own ring, a slim band with a single red jewel, and a plain gold one that was a little too big for her finger.

"Ready to get started?" Carlene asked brightly.

***

"Can we have two soups, Avrel?" Frankie called from the main part of the café.

"Give me a moment!"

Milly finished wiping a plate clean and put it in the rack to dry off. The water in the sink was getting too dirty, but she would have to be careful about using too much hot water.

"Who's the lucky person who still has to go to the Complex?" Carlene asked, walking into the kitchen with a tray of empty plates in her hands. Every week, each of the girls would spend one of their shifts helping the staff in the Complex kitchens.

"That would be me." Avrel poured a ladleful of soup into a clean white bowl. "You know, every time I go there I wonder what would happen if we got their food supply and they ended up with ours."

Milly couldn't stop herself from giggling. "Can you imagine Barton and everyone else in the Complex sitting down to eat tomato sandwiches?"

"Yes, please give our compliments to the cooks, Premier. The sandwiches were cut very well, but maybe the tomatoes could be sliced a little finer next time...oh." Avrel's smile disappeared. "Oh *no,*" she groaned.

"What's wrong?" asked Milly.

"Leo. The only visiting slot I could get this week is during my Complex shift. I can't believe I missed that!"

"Oh." An idea came to Milly. "Why don't I go instead of you? I don't mind doing two in a week."

"Really? Thanks, Milly, you're amazing." Avrel dashed over to Milly and kissed her on the cheek, beaming.

"Wasn't the order for *two* soups?" Carlene looked pointedly at the empty bowl on the side, making Avrel retreat awkwardly back to the stove.

Milly looked at the clock. Her apple and cinnamon

cake normally took thirty minutes, and there were two minutes left. She dried her hands, went to the cupboard and pulled out the cooling rack. The cake would be served warm, with a cup of tea if the customer wanted one.

"I'm closing early tonight," Carlene said. Milly stepped aside to let her plunge the used dishes into the water.

"How come?" Avrel scraped the last remnants of soup out of the pot and into a bowl. "There's not enough here for a full bowl."

"Give him three sandwiches to make up for it. Barton's going to greet the Wolf-Lords at the Complex - you know, in the Circular Hall. Do you want to go and see it? Supper won't be a problem," she added before Avrel could say anything else. "We'll just have to eat a bit earlier. Sami and Frankie said they don't mind that - what do you girls think?"

"I'd love to go," Milly said.

"I think I'll go straight home. It'll be nice having the house to myself." Avrel arranged two sandwiches on one plate, three on another and set the two bowls beside them, ready for service.

Milly took her cake out of the oven and tipped it carefully onto the cooling rack. Her mouth watered as the scent filled the kitchen. "I'll cut it up when it's cool enough."

"Thanks, Milly." Carlene picked up the tray with the soup and sandwiches and walked quickly out of the kitchen.

"Any chance you could sneak a few slices for us?" Avrel asked mischievously. Milly laughed, shaking her head. That was against the rules in Layden's and they both knew it. Customers got food first, then Carlene and the girls.

Sometimes Carlene would make an exception, but those times were rare.

"Is it all right for you to close early?" Milly heard Sami ask. "What if we miss the drums?"

"You won't miss them," Carlene assured her. "The Wolf-Lords are going to arrive quite a while before the drums. The man sitting at that table over there earlier was a Watchman; I heard him telling his wife about it. You girls know your way back to your homes from the Complex, don't you?"

23

"Yes."

"Great! Then you've got nothing to worry about. I'm not the only business closing early today."

The rest of the day seemed to drag by. Milly's cake slowly disappeared, slice by slice, until there were only four left. Time and again she found herself glancing at the clock only to see ten minutes had passed since the last time she'd looked.

Daylight was halfway through fading when Carlene took advantage of the café's emptiness and asked what food was left. All the soup and sandwiches were gone, so Sami boiled some eggs that hadn't been set aside for cooking. Milly was still a little hungry after the egg and a slice of cake, but she didn't say anything. None of them did.

The door to the café remained unlocked, just in case somebody walked in.

"You'd better get going," Carlene said, pointing at the people walking past Layden's. All of them were going in the same direction. "They'll be here soon."

"Are you sure you're going to be OK?" Milly asked. "What if someone turns up wanting something to eat?"

"*Go.*"

Once the four girls were outside, Avrel said: "Bye. I'll see you tomorrow, all right?"

"Where else would we be?" Frankie asked, grinning. Avrel smiled back, then ran down the street, pushing past everyone heading for the Complex.

"It'll be pretty awkward if we bump into our parents if they're going as well," Frankie said as the girls began walking.

"No, it won't," Sami replied smoothly. "They won't mind if we stay with each other."

Milly knew Frankie's mother well enough to say she would mind if her daughter sat with friends instead of her. She also knew Frankie well enough not to say that.

The streets slowly became broader as they neared the Complex. This did not allow the walkers to spread out, as more and more added to the throng from different roads. Milly was forced to realise they would have been even more crowded if the city was completely populated.

They turned the final corner to see the Complex

24

looming ahead of them. Its white stones were darkened by the falling dusk, while the interior was lit with amber light that spilled out onto the street. Milly could just about see shadows flitting about inside. The main doors were thrown open, allowing the crowd to enter a large circular hallway carved out of white marble. Stairs on either side of the hallway spiralled up to balconies lying along the curves of the room; most of the crowd ignored the stairs and entered the hall itself.

The hall was the largest area in the Complex, but it wasn't all there was to it. The Complex was the largest building in Redcross, the second largest being the correction facility. It wasn't just the home of the Premier and his officials: it was also the place where they held all their meetings, made official announcements and housed important guests. The Complex was also rumoured to be the headquarters of the Watchmen.

Even though they were now inside the Complex, Frankie shivered and rubbed her hands together. "Wow, the wind's really howling out there."

"Frankie," Sami said slowly, "that's not the wind."

A chorus was floating on the air, slowly growing louder as it passed through the streets.

The girls looked at each other, then as one ran for the closest stairs, pushing their way through the people heading for the main part of the hall. When they got to the upper floor, Milly ran towards the nearest section so fast she nearly collided with the stone terrace and barely stopped herself from going over the edge. The sections were divided by marble pillars; some of the sections already had two or three people inside, watching the hall below. Milly could hear the excitement in the conversations filling the area.

"Are they here yet?" Sami peered over the edge of the balcony.

"If you were a Wolf-Lord, wouldn't you want to make the best entrance possible?" Frankie asked.

Slowly the crowd in the hall thickened until the only space of white floor left was a pathway leading up to a large table where Barton and the other officials were already seated. They watched the other end of the hall intently.

Only one seat was empty: the chair to Barton's immediate left, where the head of security usually sat. Trevel must have already left.

Before long, nobody else came through the doors. The air became stifling and heavy with apprehension and unease.

Behind the girls was a pale blue door leading to the women's suite; a dark red door was in the exact same place on the opposite balcony. Milly and the girls had never stepped inside the Red Suite, just as no man would dare go into the Blue Suite. Suites were a set of rooms set aside for rest and relaxation; before her husband's death, Carlene persuaded him to set up the unused rooms in Layden's into a Blue Suite. The rooms were furnished and kept tidy, but they had only been used three times in two years.

Barton rose from his seat and all conversation ceased, like a candle flame that had suddenly been extinguished. He walked around the table and stood before the small flight of steps leading up to it, his hands behind his back.

He nodded once.

For two minutes that felt like two hours, there was no sound at all. Then twenty figures strode in, each accompanied by a wolf walking at his or her side.

Every single human was wearing a black scarf.

This wasn't real. This wasn't happening.

Milly's fingers gripped the balustrade as the Wolf-Lords walked further and further into the hall.

She noticed who was leading them. His wolf was an adult now, her black fur almost taking on a silvery tinge in the light. He walked as purposefully as she did; neither took their eyes off the Premier.

"Him?" Sami whispered. "*He's* the leader now?"

Milly didn't know his name. She had never even thought to ask it.

There was a flurry of movement as Frankie ran from the balcony. None of the other watchers seemed to have even noticed she was gone. Milly heard the Blue Suite door bang open, but she didn't turn around. She couldn't.

"Good evening!" Premier Barton called, his voice echoing through the hall. "It's an honour to welcome you here, Wolf-Lord Andras."

The black-haired Wolf-Lord reached the bottom of the

steps. Then he began to walk up them with slow, deliberate paces. The watching crowd drew in a shocked breath and Milly thought she saw the expression on Barton's face flicker slightly. He stepped back a few paces and then Andras stood on the landing before him.

Andras nodded his head once in reply. "Thank you, Premier Barton. It's an honour to be here."

"May I offer my sincere condolences on the death of your predecessor?" Barton asked.

"Thank you," Andras replied smoothly, "and we're grateful for your hospitality."

"Do you wish to make any changes to the terms?" "If they're still acceptable to you, there's no need to change them."

"Everyone," Barton said loudly, "please join me in welcoming the Andras Wolf-Lords to Redcross!"

The circular hall of the Complex erupted in cheers and claps.

Milly looked at Sami, the icy fear coursing through her reflected in the other girl's eyes.

"Where's Frankie?" asked Sami, her voice a hoarse whisper. Barton was speaking again. Nobody was looking at the girls.

"She went through here." Milly headed towards the Blue Suite and pushed the door open. The walls of the Suite were cerulean, with cushions the colour of a spring sky positioned neatly on soft navy chairs. A painting of crashing waves hung on the wall next to a door that was painted a pure, clean white.

"Frankie? Are you all right?" Milly called, looking around to see if her friend was hiding anywhere.

There was the unmistakable sound of someone rinsing their mouth out and spitting in a sink. The white door opened and Frankie emerged, her face grey. She glanced wildly around before leaning in close and whispering:

"What are we going to *do?*"

Milly said the first words that came into her head. "We stay calm," she said. "We stay calm and keep out of their way."

"It won't be easy avoiding a group of people in a city with a wall surrounding it!" Frankie cried.

"Shh!" Sami hissed, gesturing towards the door of the

27

Blue Suite.

"Sorry. But seriously, how easy is it to walk down a couple of streets without bumping into a Watchman or someone on the security team? And do you really think the wolves aren't going to notice how scared we are?"

"They won't. Think about it. They are going to be surrounded by people who've probably never even *seen* a wolf before. Why would the wolves pick out our fear from the crowd? All we have to do is stay away from them as much as we can." Milly looked at both of her friends. "Someone told me not to be fearful around Wolf-Lords or their wolves. If we do, they're going to think we're prey."

Frankie nodded shakily. "Like I said, it's not going to be easy."

"I think we can do it," Sami said. "They won't be here forever."

Chapter 3

Two Years Ago

The next stop on the journey was a cluster of islands, known collectively as the Gull Islands. Milly waited with the other travellers for Weatherhill to return with the new group of emigrants. Her feet ached slightly; she leaned against the nearest tree to take a little pressure off them.

"How many do you think she'll come back with?" she asked Samara.

"Depends how many have to leave. There are eight islands, so there might be a lot."

Milly was about to ask her what she meant by having to leave when Weatherhill strode into the trees, her wolf at her side. Behind her was a group of about fifteen people, all wearing warm but rough-looking clothes.

One of them caught Milly's eye right away. She was impossible to miss, and not just because she was the only newcomer wearing something red. Her hair was dark and wild, and she couldn't stop looking around as if wanting to remember everything she saw.

As soon as the girl saw Milly and Samara watching, she raised a hand and waved to them, a huge grin on her face.

When it was time to eat, Samara and Milly chose to sit with each other rather than with their families. This time, the meat was fresh and roasted over fires. Milly and Samara were just getting their share when the girl from the Gull Islands hurried over to them.

"Hi. I'm Frankie Jamison." Her hazel eyes sparkled playfully, and she had a small turned-up nose.

"I'm Milly Costello and this is..." Milly trailed off awkwardly. "I'm sorry - I never asked your last name."

"Morel," Samara announced. "Samara Morel."

"What's 'Milly' short for?" asked Frankie. "Is that short for something, or is that your actual name?"

"My full name's Emilia. Spelled E-M-I-L-I-A."

"*My* full name's Francesca, but only two people call me that. One's my mum and the other one hates me." Her red jumper was baggy; it hung loose on her shoulders and

29

around her wrists.

"Why does she hate you?" Samara asked.

Now Frankie looked a little uncomfortable. "He. Let's just say there was an incident at the school. I wasn't involved, but he kept watching me afterwards even though he knew it wasn't me. It felt really strange."

"That doesn't mean he hates you," Milly said.

"Francesca!" yelled a voice. Frankie winced.

"I have to go. See you!" With that, she took the bowl one of the cooks was holding out to her and fled. She rejoined them on the march an hour later.

**

Like all Fearainn cities, Redcross was built with a wall around it for protection. Unfortunately, as some cities discovered, walls trapped the people inside just as much as they protected them. Once a weakness was found in the wall, the rest of the city was left almost defenceless.

They also left the cities isolated from the world outside. Villages didn't have that weakness. Towns - also known as open towns - were left without a wall even after the wars, when it was certain there was no further danger to them. Another advantage was towns could be expanded; if a Premier wanted to add more buildings to a city that was already crowded, he or she would have to knock down part of the wall and wait until the buildings were complete before rebuilding the wall, which would leave the city vulnerable. The only other choice was knock down older houses and build new ones.

Premiers never considered the greatest threat to a city could come from inside the wall, or from something the city desperately needed. Cholera rushed through the city of Redcross like a flood, sweeping away over half of the population and leaving the place with a feeling of emptiness.

Barton was elected Premier because he was one of the few people who stepped in to take charge and purify the water system. The first thing he did after his election was impose a curfew. His reason was that a lot of houses had been burgled after their owners had been reported deceased, and the city would be safer at night if nobody roamed the streets and caused trouble after sunset. Barton also announced that there would be a special force to patrol the streets at night; they would make sure citizens stayed behind closed doors, as they were supposed to.

The second thing he did was recruit men into his special force, called the Watchmen. The third was to send letters out to all the cities and towns, inviting people to travel to Redcross and start a new life.

The curfew was met with deep resentment from the older citizens. As the weeks passed, they realised Barton wasn't going to relent no matter how much they protested. It took a few arrests by the Watchmen to make them understand he was serious.

Barton didn't take the younger citizens into account.

It was Jason Rowe who began the tradition of 'running'. He watched until he knew precisely when the Watchmen would be passing down his street. The following night, he crept out of his house at just the right time and ran through the streets, keeping well out of the way of the black-clad Watchmen.

Success made him confident, and he started to creep out again and again. He told his friends how easy it was to elude the Watchmen, which prompted them to make their own attempts. Some of them weren't as careful as Jason. The 'runners' who remained free knew there wasn't any proof they had been out after curfew other than the word of others. The Redcross security team were always reluctant to arrest anyone without proof, and runners didn't betray each other.

The normal sentence for breaking curfew once was two months in the facility; if you were caught a second time, two more months were added and so on. When Leo da Lange was captured on his first run, he was offered a deal: give names of other runners and have a day taken off for each one or keep quiet and serve a year. He chose to serve a year.

The new arrivals learned one thing very quickly: if they didn't pull their weight in Redcross, they didn't eat. It was that simple. If they were able to work, they did, regardless of what the job was and even if they were only marginally good at it. If they weren't, that wasn't a problem. They were very quick learners.

31

***

Now

"Where's Avrel?" Milly tied her fleece around her waist and looked around the small kitchen. Once they started cooking, the room would become warm very quickly.

"She's not here yet. Could you slice these loaves for me, please? We're doing sausage and egg sandwiches this morning; the delivery came this morning."

"Sure." Milly took the breadknife out of the drawer. The top of the first loaf felt as hard as stone on her first try, but she gripped the knife tighter and sawed through the bread. The first slice was ragged and uneven.

Frankie was already cooking the sausages. She smiled awkwardly at Milly before turning back to the frying-pan.

"What did Avrel say when you called?" Milly asked.

"She wanted to know how we could *act natural* while the Wolf-Lords are here. I said we'd just have to do what we always do. It shouldn't be that hard, right? Just avoid the Wolf-Lords and everything's going to be fine."

As if sensing they'd been discussing her, Avrel walked into Layden's. Her yellow scarf was tied around her neck and her hair was wild and loose. She looked agitated and angry.

"Good thing I'm not putting *you* in the kitchen today," Carlene remarked. "Can you put these forks out?"

She pressed a cluster of forks into Avrel's hands and turned away. Avrel stared down at the cutlery before arranging them on the tables.

By the time Milly finished the first still-warm loaf, Frankie was beginning to start frying the eggs. Once the sausages and eggs were inside the buttered slices of bread, they would cause the butter to melt deliciously.

"Tell me about last evening." Carlene stood in the kitchen doorway, watching as Milly cut slices of bread from the still-warm loaf in front of her. The arrival of the Wolf-Lords hadn't been broadcast because it wasn't an announcement. "Are the Andras Wolf-Lords like the ones who escorted you?"

"They're the same ones." Milly tried to sound as if she

wasn't remotely bothered by that.

"Oh, so they've got a new leader. He must have hated standing at the bottom of those steps."

"He didn't," Milly said. "He walked right up them." To her surprise, her voice carried more than a little admiration.

"He did *what*?" Carlene laughed out loud.

"He wasn't meant to do that?" Frankie asked.

"Nobody does that! When Barton greets someone formally, he stands at the top of the steps with the guest at the bottom."

"That means he's always looking down at them," said Milly.

By walking up the steps, Andras was saying Barton wasn't to look down on him or at him, that they were equals and should speak as such. Either that, or he had no idea what his action implied.

Milly wondered if Weatherhill would have known exactly what the implications were and if she would have done it anyway.

She concentrated on the other things Carlene asked her to do for the rest of the morning, all the while aware of the others coming and going while carrying an air of cold tension around with them. Every time the door to Layden's opened she would glance towards it, terrified she would see a tall figure with a wolf beside it step into the café.

"You know, you girls have been a bit on edge today," Carlene remarked as soon as the café was empty after lunchtime. "You've hardly even talked to each other. Is everything OK?"

"Yeah, everything's fine." Frankie sounded far too nonchalant.

Milly bit her lip. If Carlene noticed something wasn't right, their parents certainly would. They needed to be more careful.

"Is it the Wolf-Lords? You were all right before they arrived, so why are you planning to avoid them? I could hear Frankie and Milly talking; that's what happens when you leave the kitchen door open." She frowned, studying each girl in turn. "Why are all of you so jumpy about the Wolf-Lords?"

The girls looked at each other, unease slowly giving

way to resignation.

"Let's just say we might have liberated something from them last time." Frankie couldn't quite meet Carlene's eyes.

Carlene raised her eyebrows. "You *might* have?"

"We definitely liberated something," Avrel admitted sheepishly.

"And you got away with it? Yes, you really could be in trouble for that, couldn't you?"

"Please." Milly stepped forward. She kept her voice soft, knowing if she raised it her desperation would be clear. "Please don't tell them."

"It's OK," Carlene said, raising both hands soothingly. "I won't tell them. I'm going to leave that up to you."

"Why?" asked Sami.

Carlene shrugged in reply. "It's not my secret to tell. Like I said, how you deal with it is entirely up to you. Now I need someone to..."

She went on talking about the food to be prepared for supper, but Milly was only half-listening. Carlene said she wouldn't tell the Wolf-Lords the girls had a secret...so why didn't Milly feel more relieved?

***

Branches snapped under Milly's feet. Her breath was coming too fast and it burned her lungs. She could barely see where she was going. She ran through the trees, darting through gaps between them. She heard leaves swishing beside her and over her head, but she kept running.

She swerved roughly to avoid colliding with a tree; she didn't even feel the bark scrape her palms as she pushed herself away from the trunk.

Eventually she reached a stone wall and collapsed against it, frantically gulping in air. Leaves were still rustling; she could hear them everywhere, especially in the branches above her.

Then the howls started. They pierced the night like shards of glass. Sound bled into Milly's ears and she started running again. Her feet slapped heavily on cobblestones as she passed under a lamp's pale glow. She knew where she was now. If she kept going, she'd reach home and then she'd be safe.

The howls were louder now, filling the streets like an angry song. Milly thought she could hear human footsteps behind her now, but she couldn't let that stop her...

Her eyes flew open. The footsteps were real. They were real, and they were getting closer.

She scrambled out of bed and over to the window, throwing the curtains open just in time to see lithe shapes run down the small street. Human figures ran alongside and after them. Close behind them were two men with torches that sent orange beams through the darkness.

Watchmen were recognisable in any light.

Her phone trilled. Milly tore her eyes away from the disappearing shapes and hurried towards the wall, thankful for the thickness of the floor between her bedroom and her parents'. She pulled the phone out of its receiver. "Hello?"

"Have you seen them?" It was Avrel. "Sorry - of course you did. The whole of Redcross probably knows about them." Watchmen usually patrolled the streets in pairs, not groups. "Why have they got the wolves with them?"

"I think they're hunting."

"But there's no prey around here."

"Yes, there is." Milly went back to the window and stared at the house opposite her, lit by the meagre light outside. "Remember Barton said he'd made a deal about the security of Redcross? I think he was talking about the runners. They're the greatest threat to security inside the city right now."

"Forgive me if I don't feel too sorry for them." Avrel hung up. Milly stayed by the window, feeling the cold outside through the thin glass.

If Jason and the other runners could break curfew regularly and get away with it, what could other people do if they thought they could escape consequences?

The worst thing was, the runners knew so much about the Watchmen's schedule that this was going to come as a complete surprise to them.

She heard a shriek in the distance.

Chapter 4

Two Years Ago

"Wait, why are we going back?" Frankie asked in bewilderment. Weatherhill was leading the travellers, including the new arrivals, away from the small lake where they'd been waiting and back the way they had come. "Jack and I looked up routes we might take to get to Redcross. The fastest way is to keep going the way we were and through this wood; that way, it'll only take us a few more days."

Ahead of them, the black-haired Wolf-Lord ran to catch up with Weatherhill, his wolf loping at his side. He began to talk to Weatherhill in a low voice; she answered him, but she didn't stop walking.

"Fancy going up and telling *her* that?" Samara gestured towards Weatherhill.

Frankie shook her head. "Not really."

"Look over there," Milly whispered, nodding towards a young woman walking beside one of the Wolf-Lords. "She's not with us, is she? She's not a traveller?"

"No, she's definitely one of them," Samara replied. "Ours was the first town they stopped at; I know I'd recognise her if she came from there. Look, she's even dressed like they are."

"Where's her wolf?" Milly asked. When her friends said nothing, she went on: "I'm serious. There are twelve Wolf-Lords but only eleven wolves. Count them."

Frankie did so quickly, her eyes widening when she got to the end. "You're right. She doesn't have one."

"Enough!" Weatherhill was now glaring at the younger Wolf-Lord; her wolf snarled, baring its fangs. After a moment, the male Wolf-Lord bowed his head and moved away. Weatherhill watched him go, her eyes like ice. Then she began walking again.

"Talk about tense."

Two olive-skinned teenagers had approached without the girls noticing. They looked about a year or so older than Milly, Samara and Frankie. One, a boy with dark brown hair and eyes, grinned at them. "I'm Leo. This is my little sister Avrel."

"Really?" said Frankie. "You look the same age."

"We're twins," Avrel replied. Her hair was a lot lighter than her brother's; it was brown and curly, with a few stray hairs hanging about her face. Around her neck was a small green scarf. "He was born first and he's never let me forget it."

"My name's Milly." Milly hopped neatly over a small rock that was in her way.

"I'm Frankie, and I guess that makes her Sami!" Frankie said brightly, squeezing Samara's shoulder.

"Call me Avvy and you die," Avrel warned. But she was smiling.

"What do you know about Redcross?" asked Leo. He sounded as if he was genuinely curious about the place, and not like he wanted to compare his knowledge with theirs.

"Not much," Milly admitted reluctantly. "Just that it's a city that was half-emptied after an illness. I don't even know when it was founded." She realised she could have asked Susanna to find a few things out - but then, her sister had enough studies to deal with.

"Me neither!" Leo laughed.

"I tried looking it up, but I couldn't find anything important. Just references and comparisons to other cities." Sami's hands rested casually in her fleece pockets. Her hair was tangled from the wind; Milly reminded herself to give Sami something to tie it back - if she had something Sami could use.

"Really? Where'd you go, your family's library?" Leo asked jokingly. Then he saw Sami's face had gone bright red. "Wait. You actually did that?"

"Your family's got a library?" Frankie cried.

"Yes. We did." Sami's smile was as sharp as a knife.

There was silence for a while after that. Then Leo spoke again. "So we've got some extra days travelling to do. Hope Weatherhill knows what she's doing."

"Barton asked her to escort us. Why wouldn't she know what she's doing?" The second Frankie finished saying those words, an uneasy expression came over her face.

Milly knew what she was thinking. The Wolf-Lords

were the only protection the travellers had. If anything happened on the journey, who would know and who would care?

***

Now

Milly sensed sunlight dancing on her bedroom wall. She opened her eyes to see blue and pale gold through a small gap in her curtains. After listening to the wolves, she had fallen asleep with howls still echoing in her dreams, yet she wasn't tired.

She glanced at her tiny clock. Curfew had finished literally a minute ago; everything would be peaceful outside.

She threw the covers aside and got dressed in her pink dress and sandals as quickly and as quietly as she could. She was glad her sandals had soft soles. It was easy to be woken up by Watchmen running past your window.

Creeping softly down the stairs, she reached the front door and opened it, stepping out into the morning. The walk would only be a short one; she would be back before it was time to go to work.

Cold air hit her arms and legs. She shivered but stepped into the beam of warmth falling across the street.

There was nobody around, not even the Watchmen. Milly began to walk, not quite sure where she was going or even if she wanted to go anywhere.

Everything was so quiet, so peaceful. Redcross was bathed in morning sunlight; Milly could hear birds singing outside and inside the walls. She kept looking up at the sky in the hope that the moon would still be there, a pale sliver of white in the sea of blue.

Before she realised where she was going, she found herself standing right in the middle of the area where the market was held twice a week. In Redcross, there were four main roads that divided the city into sections; the shape the roads made was what gave the city its name. The roads met precisely in the centre of Redcross, forming a large square. Milly could go anywhere from here. If she

38

kept walking, she'd end up passing Layden's; if she turned right, she would eventually reach the main gates.

Would they let her out?

Milly's insides fluttered. Could she persuade the guards to let her leave Redcross for a few minutes? The hills and trees would be beautiful in the light and Milly hadn't been outside the city for a long time.

If she didn't go now, she might lose her chance.

She turned right, and nearly screamed. Two wolves stood in front of her, watching her intently. One was coal-black with eyes like smouldering embers; the other had red fur tipped with grey.

Milly kept very still, heart hammering. Making eye contact was a big mistake with wild creatures. She forced herself to look at the tips of their ears.

These weren't wild wolves.

The red wolf stepped up to her. Milly shuddered as she felt hot breath on the side of her right hand. The red wolf sniffed her hand once, then stepped away from her. The black wolf stayed where it was for a moment before padding away back down the street.

"Hello."

The red wolf's ears twitched; it trotted past Milly, its fur brushing against her fingers. Milly looked over her shoulder to see a young Wolf-Lord standing behind her, scratching the back of the red wolf's neck. He seemed to be waiting for something.

Then she realised he hadn't been talking to the wolf. "Hi," she replied.

"You were part of the emigration, weren't you?" His dark brown hair was slightly longer than most men in Redcross wore theirs.

"Yes." Milly shouldn't have been surprised he remembered her, even though she, along with pretty much everyone else in the convoy, had gone out of her way not to talk to the Wolf-Lords escorting them. The Wolf-Lords hadn't spoken to them either.

The wolf almost looked like a large dog standing beside his master. But the Wolf-Lords weren't masters of the wolves and they weren't friends either. From what she had read, they were more like one soul sharing two bodies.

Would the wolf tear her to shreds if he asked it to?

"What's your name?" he asked.

Milly swallowed, trying to moisten her dry throat. "I'm Emilia."

"I'm Alasdair." He laid his hand gently on the wolf's head. "And this guy here is Conall."

"Hi, Conall," Milly said - and then stopped in embarrassment. Conall wasn't a person. Why was she talking to him as if he were human?

"What are you doing out here so early?" Now Alasdair was frowning. "Do you have to be somewhere?"

Was he accusing her of breaking curfew? No, he couldn't be. She was wearing sandals and a dress; nobody wore those clothes to deliberately break curfew. "Not yet. I just wanted to walk around for a bit while everything was so quiet." It sounded like a flimsy reason now that she'd spoken it. "I'm actually going home now."

She needed to get back to the house and change her clothes; she couldn't work in Layden's wearing her dress, even though the day was getting warmer.

She could feel the sun's rays touching her arms.

"Would you feel safer if we walked you home?"

Milly was so surprised, she couldn't respond for a moment. What could she do? She wanted to say no but didn't want to risk offending the Wolf-Lord. It wasn't just because of the wolf: he and the others were invited to Redcross by the Premier himself and offending the Premier's guest was not a good idea.

"Thank you," she said.

"Does that mean you mind, or you don't?"

"I don't mind. My home's this way." She began walking back the way she'd come; after a moment, Conall caught up with her and walked beside her. If Milly didn't look at the wolf, she could almost imagine he wasn't there.

It was impossible - and rude - to pretend Alasdair wasn't there. "You're staying in the Complex, aren't you?" The Premier always had rooms set aside for his personal guests. Wolf-Lords wouldn't be any different. "How do you like it?" She tried to keep her voice light and indifferent.

"I don't know. It's different. There's not a lot of space here - open space, I mean." Alasdair put a hand to his mouth to stifle a yawn. "It's like being shut away from everywhere. Sorry," he added quickly.

"It's OK," Milly said. They *were* shut away from everywhere. She wasn't going to deny that.

"Was it different for you too?" Alasdair asked. "Where did you come from before you moved here?"

"Kindainn."

"An open town? Yeah, that is different." Wolf-Lords lived in villages; Milly wasn't sure why they were called that as some of them were rumoured to be just as large as open towns. "We collected you from so many places, but we never got to see any of them. Could you tell me what Kindainn's like?"

"Well, it's..." Milly's memories caught her throat. She couldn't think how to describe it. She looked up at the sky and tried to picture Kindainn on a perfect spring day, or when the carnival visited in the summer and the air echoed with laughter. "It's beautiful, and I'm not just saying that. There are three rivers; well, they're more like streams but we call them rivers. Two of them run right through the town and the third goes right past it. We swam in them when it was warm enough. Every single house has wild roses growing right in front of it; the Mayor's house is practically surrounded by roses and they are so gorgeous when they're in full bloom. We lived in a very pretty house. It wasn't as big as the Mayor's, but it was enough for us."

Her eyes stung. She blinked fiercely.

"Was it just you and your parents?"

Milly shook her head. "I've got two sisters. They moved out before we did. Have you got brothers and sisters?"

"Nope. Well, I guess I do. You know how a pack is a family? Once you bond with a wolf cub, you become part of that family. Got to keep on the right side of the wolf in charge, though."

Milly hadn't known Weatherhill personally, but from what she'd seen of her, keeping on Weatherhill's good side was very sensible.

"What happened to her?" she asked.

Alasdair pressed his lips together and looked at the ground. "She fell."

"I'm sorry." A breeze suddenly blew down the street, ruffling Milly's hair.

"Are you cold?" Alasdair asked.

"I can handle it."

41

Milly had probably missed breakfast by now; her mother might not be very happy when she got back home.

"This is my home," she said once they were outside the Costellos' front door. "Thanks for walking me back."

"You're welcome."

Milly was just about to open the door when he spoke again. "I just remembered - you didn't say your last name."

"Oh. It's Costello." Although Wolf-Lords had surnames, they almost never went by them. The only time a Wolf-Lord was called by his or her last name was on becoming a leader.

Then Milly's gaze fell on Conall again - and she remembered exactly who she was talking to and who she had been walking with. "Goodbye."

She went inside and shut the door behind her.

Chapter 5

Everyone in Fearainn called the battles between *teaghlachs* 'the wars', although most of them had been violent arguments over land that ended in severe injuries to both humans and wolves. The true war began because of the brutality of a single Wolf-Lord.

Each Wolf-Lord *teaghlach* had its own village, and a large section of land surrounding it. As each *teaghlach* grew larger and larger, they needed more territory to support themselves and the other villagers. They expanded their borders until they were dangerously close to open towns, who had no interest in being taken over by Wolf-Lords.

The trouble was, it wasn't just Wolf-Lords they had to contend with. They also had to deal with the wolves. When faced a solemn-faced messenger, with a wolf standing beside him, most Mayors or Mayoresses chose to yield and the town became the property of the *teaghlach*.

One Wolf-Lord was expanding the borders of his land faster than the others. Joshua Haigan was the leader of the largest *teaghlach* in Fearainn, and he didn't care if he had to take over land owned by Mayors or Premiers as long as he got the land itself. Cities were safe behind their high walls, but open towns were left undefended. Several Premiers weren't interested in helping the towns – after all, wolves couldn't breach city walls. Why open the doors and leave the city open to a takeover?

Eventually, the inevitable happened: Haigan started to take over land owned by other Wolf-Lords. The first protest was swiftly and mercilessly silenced. Haigan destroyed two more *teaghlachs*, their villages and an open town before anyone realised what was happening.

Terrified her town would be next, the Mayoress of Ardlaig sent out as many messengers as she could, warning other settlements of the threat.

The remaining *teaghlachs* – including the ones who were also expanding their land – were outraged. Arguments and fights over territory boundaries were permitted; an outright takeover was not. Just because the

Wolf-Lords were bonded with wolves did not mean they had to act like them. They were also afraid, because no Wolf-Lord had ever attacked a settlement before and Haigan had taken over a quarter of Fearainn. If he went on like this, he could become the ruler of the entire land.

The Wolf-Lords banded together into a single warband and took a stand against Haigan.

People always shuddered when they read stories of the battles that followed. The war only ended when a member of Haigan's own *teaghlach* suddenly turned on him before another battle could begin and forced a stalemate. The survivors disappeared back to their own lands, with a promise that the borders would return to their original size - for a while.

Every single leader who took part in the wars was painted beside a wolf that had blood oozing from its mouth. Joshua Haigan was always depicted as a dark shadow in front of a burning village, with corpses sprawled out behind him and a snarling monster at his side.

***

Dressed in warmer clothes, Milly arrived at Layden's to find her friends already there. "Sorry I'm late," she said.

"Don't worry about it," Carlene replied. "Just don't make it a habit, all right?"

"I won't." Luckily, there were no customers around. Milly started putting out knives and forks while Avrel took out a small selection of cups for tea.

"How's Leo?" Frankie asked as she emerged from the kitchen, wiping flour from her hands. "I bet you're looking forward to seeing him later."

"We got a letter from the facility day before yesterday. Leo's allowed unsupervised visits now," Avrel announced.

"You don't sound happy about it," Sami remarked. "Doesn't that mean he's earning privileges?"

"He is. Now he gets two visits." Avrel looked as if she was about to start crying. "And our parents still won't go and see him. It's like they want to pretend he doesn't even exist!"

"I'm sure they don't," Milly began, not sure what else to say.

"So why aren't they visiting him? He's stopped asking if they're going to see him, but he still asks after them and all I can say is *fine*. Thing is, if the same person visits an inmate too many times, the guards start to get suspicious."

"But you visited him before and..." Frankie's face fell. "Oh. Those were supervised."

"Exactly. Family visits are OK, but more than one a week and they'll start thinking we're planning an escape. I'm not joking about that."

Suddenly she went still and looked over to where Sami stood in the kitchen doorway. "Leo gets to visit the library without a guard now."

"That's great," Sami said.

"There are old books there," Avrel continued. "I mean, very old books. Books your family would have loved to have in the library you left behind, and probably twice as rare."

"You don't need to bribe me, Avrel. Leo's my friend too, even though I don't think I've ever said it out loud before, and I'd love to visit him."

"And you get access to the library," Frankie pointed out, grinning playfully, "and that *cultural improvement* thing they've got going on in the facility."

"Can someone check the porridge?" Carlene yelled, pointing towards the pan on the stove. Frankie's shoes skidded on the kitchen floor as she went to rescue the oatmeal from bubbling over.

"Shall I get out the honey or the jam?" Milly asked Carlene. Some customers liked to have a little jam or honey on their porridge, just like she did.

"Just the honey. I'm saving the jam for something. Don't forget, you're going to the Complex this afternoon."

***

Milly was no longer nervous about walking down a tiny alley to the small door reserved for cooks and the Premier's other servants. She pushed the door open as confidently as if the Complex had been her own house and stepped inside.

"Milly!" Joyce was the head cook of the Complex; she always smelled of freshly baked bread. Nearby, a kitchen assistant named Kaleb was using a cleaver to chop raw meat. "What are you doing here? Avrel's down for today, not you."

"We swapped shifts." Identical aprons hung from pegs just beside the door. Milly reached for the nearest one and slipped it over her head. "I know we should have told you, but this was the only chance for her to see Leo this week."

"Actually, you should take that off."

Confused, Milly did as Joyce said. "Is there a problem?"

"You don't want the Premier to see you in an apron, sweetheart."

Milly's world jolted sharply. "The Premier wants to see me?"

No. They couldn't have told him.

As if sensing Milly wasn't able to move by herself, Joyce put a hand on her shoulder and gently moved her towards a nearby flight of steps. Milly wasn't sure how she managed to walk up them, but she kept going, strangely reassured by Joyce's hand.

The Premier's office was on the highest floor of the Complex. Joyce escorted Milly to the door and left her there with one last comforting squeeze to her shoulder.

Milly raised a hand and knocked. The sound seemed to echo. She instinctively stepped backwards.

"Come in!" Premier Barton's voice echoed through the wood.

Milly tried to move, but her ribs felt too tight. Her back and arms prickled. The doorknob was cold against her palm.

She grasped it firmly and opened the door.

"Ah, you must be Miss Costello!"

Premier Barton was seated at his desk. Milly concentrated on looking at him and not the imposing figure of Andras standing just to his left. "I'm afraid I have a favour to ask of you. Some of the council members are uncomfortable with having wolves in the meeting. Could you go to the kitchens, find Kaleb and take the meat he gives you to the wolves?"

"Yes, Premier."

"You'll find them in the Lower Balcony room. Oh, and we need you to sit with them until the meeting's over. Can

46

you do that?"

Milly swallowed. It took all her willpower not to flinch or show fear, even as it clutched her heart. "I can." She didn't remember going down to the kitchen, talking to Kaleb and collecting the bucket of raw meat. She didn't feel the handle of the bucket as it dug a groove into her skin. All she could think of was that she didn't need to be scared, she wasn't prey.

Emilia Costello was not prey.

The door to the Lower Balcony room was in front of her. She gripped the bucket handle until her knuckles hurt and took deep breaths into her lungs. She wouldn't have to stay with them for long; it would only be for an hour. That was how long normal meetings lasted, or so she'd been told.

It wasn't the wolves she was afraid of.

The lower balcony room was made from a darker stone than the rest of the Complex; the only light came through two windows set high in the wall and fell on the five wolves sitting patiently on the floor. Milly recognised two of them from the market: the black wolf and Conall. Two grey wolves sat side by side, with Andras' wolf a short way away from them.

There weren't any plates or bowls in the room, and Milly hadn't been given any. She put the bucket down, wincing at the loud clang the metal made on the marble before kneeling beside it. How was she supposed to feed them?

As Andras' wolf padded up to her, she understood exactly how.

"You're Aela, aren't you?"

The she-wolf gave no response to her name. She regarded Milly with beautiful silver eyes. Very slowly, Milly picked up a steak and held it out, palm open. Aela gracefully picked it up in her jaws, then stalked away and sat down to devour it.

The black wolf was the next to approach, eyes almost glowing in the half-light. The two greys and Conall patiently waited their turn. Milly didn't know much about wolves, but she was aware there was a hierarchy of some kind in packs. Did the Wolf-Lords affect the position of the wolf in the pack? Or was it the other way around?

Weatherhill's wolf - Milly had no idea whether it was male or female - had clearly been just as much in charge as Weatherhill herself was.

Milly's palms were cold. She looked down and saw a sticky sheen of blood covering them.

Aela stood before her again. Milly held her empty hands out; Aela studied them for a moment before putting a paw on Milly's knees and sniffing her face and around her left ear. Milly held her head up. She wondered if the she-wolf could hear her heart beating.

Aela's teeth were so, so close.

One moment Milly was kneeling on the marble floor, the next she was lying on her back with Aela's nose just touching her throat.

Milly couldn't move. She fixed her eyes on the ceiling, barely able to see it past the fur on Aela's shoulder. She didn't want to die like this. She didn't want to die at all.

A warm, rough tongue moved over her cheek twice.

Teeth scraped at the side of her head, then Aela was gone. After a moment, Milly slowly sat up and watched as the wolves wrestled and played with each other. One of the grey wolves started to chase Conall around the room, staying behind him but not quite close enough to catch his tail. Conall kept looking back, as if hoping the other wolf hadn't given up on the game.

The second grey continued to wrestle with the black wolf. They snapped at each other's muzzles, growling heavily. After a moment the grey was on its back, trying to push the black's muzzle away from its face with its front paws. Milly looked at Aela but the she-wolf was completely unconcerned, choosing instead to keep an eye on Conall and the first grey.

Milly clapped her hands sharply. Immediately five pairs of glowing eyes focused on her. The wolves watched her silently, expectantly, waiting to see what she would do. Embarrassed, Milly lowered her hands and put them on the floor. It wasn't her place to interfere. It was Aela's.

"I'm sorry," she said.

Aela huffed in reply.

***

48

"How's Leo?" Sami asked as soon as Avrel walked inside Layden's.

"He's fine," Avrel replied. "He's looking forward to seeing you; we booked a slot for you tomorrow. I know it's really short notice - again - but all the later ones were already taken."

"Oh, that's all right. I don't mind." "I thought you wouldn't."

Milly smiled to herself. Avrel's smile and eyes were a little brighter than they had been the previous day.

The door opened. "Excuse me?"

Everyone turned to see a Watchman standing in the doorway. He was in his late twenties or early thirties, with short brown hair that had clearly been carefully groomed.

"Hi," he said. "I'm looking for Emilia." Before Milly got a chance to speak, he spotted her and smiled apologetically. "Sorry - *you're* Emilia. Premier Barton's asked for you."

"How come? She was at the Complex yesterday," Frankie said.

"Turns out she did such a good job feeding the wolves yesterday, the Premier wants her to do it again." The Watchman never took his eyes from Milly as he spoke.

Frankie stared at Milly in surprise, as did Sami and Avrel.

"I don't know why, the Wolf-Lords are perfectly capable of feeding their own wolves, but it's Premier's orders. If you'd like to get your coat, you'll be back here before lunch."

Lunchtime was when Layden's had the most customers and Carlene needed the girls to help prepare food and clean up afterwards.

"You'd better get going," Carlene said.

Milly untied her apron and hung it back up in the kitchen. "I'll be back soon," she promised her friends before following the Watchman out into the street.

"Sorry about this," the Watchman said as soon as the door was shut. "If it's a choice between working in Layden's or having to feed wolves, I know what I'd rather be doing."

"It wasn't so bad. They didn't try to bite me. Is Barton holding another meeting?" Milly asked, looking up at the

Watchman as they walked.

"I don't think so. They don't need you to feed the wolves, they just want you to. The wolves are back in the Lower Balcony room; you remember where that is?"

Milly nodded.

"Good. Kaleb's got the meat, so just collect it from him and do what you did last time."

When they neared the Complex, Milly was about to head for the small alley when the Watchman said: "You don't have to do that. You're doing a favour for the Wolf-Lords and the Premier."

"It's the quickest way to the kitchen," Milly pointed out.

"Then I'll walk you to the door. Barton said to make sure you got there, and I do not want to get on the wrong side of the new head of security."

"Is he here?" Milly asked.

"Yeah. Haven't met him yet, but apparently he's, uh..." The Watchman half-laughed, raising his eyebrows at the same time. "Sorry - I shouldn't talk like this about my new boss, even if he is only temporary." There was just enough space in the alley for them to walk side by side. "He's from the Gull Islands. Ever heard of them?"

"I've got a friend from there."

"He was personally recommended by Trevel herself," he said grandly, as if making an announcement to the entire circular hall, "so he's got to have something about him if she asked him to travel from way over there."

Eventually, they reached the wooden door. The Watchman gestured towards it. "Thank you for your company on this rather short walk. If you get torn to pieces, I'll help your family avenge your death."

With one last smile, he was gone.

Milly opened the door and was hit with the smell of meat cooking. She wondered how the Premier was going to be able to keep feeding the wolves; she wasn't sure just what kind of meat was being used, but it wasn't chicken, which was easiest to get hold of.

Kaleb was at the table in the centre of the kitchen, peeling carrots and setting them aside in a neat pile.

At the opposite end of the table, Joyce was doing the same thing with some green and red apples. She glanced up as Milly entered.

"Hello, sweetheart!"

"Hi, Joyce."

Kaleb put down his knife and went over to the fridge. He opened it and, with a grunt of effort, took out two buckets and carried them over to Milly. "There you go. Know where you're going?"

"I do. Thanks."

The buckets were almost overflowing with raw meat. Milly's stomach clenched: there was far too much for five wolves. She took the buckets and left the kitchen, determined not to stagger under the weight. She'd carried heavier things before.

She opened the door to the Lower Balcony room to find all twenty wolves waiting for her.

For a moment, she stood still. Then Milly set the buckets down; the sound of metal hitting marble jarred the air unpleasantly. Milly knelt beside the bucket, picked up a slab of meat and waited for Aela to approach.

After Aela took her portion, the other wolves stepped forward, one by one. The black wolf waited until eight other wolves had eaten before its turn. Sometimes, a wolf's teeth scraped against Milly's palm or a finger, and she barely stopped herself from pulling away. She was glad the portions were all the same size.

Conall was the last to eat. "Hi there," Milly said softly as he bent to take the food from her hands. "Where's your human?"

The wolf's ears twitched. The meat went down his throat in five snaps of his teeth; he licked his jaws, blinked and lay down right where he was, head resting on his paws. Milly got up and took two steps back from him, making sure no wolves were behind her. Slowly, she knelt back down again and rubbed her bloodstained palms against each other.

She watched as the wolves roamed around the room. They sniffed at corners and inspected the walls. Aela sat right in the centre of the room, her eyes taking in everything and her ears twitching at every noise.

Suddenly Grey One growled at another wolf, lunging at its muzzle. The other wolf leaped away and growled in reply, tail swishing from side to side. They wrestled with each other, jaws snapping and fangs grazing fur. Milly shivered, but she couldn't look away from them. She wasn't sure if she could even move.

Close by, Conall raised his head and watched the scene before him with bright eyes.

Grey One bounded away, the other wolf chasing him, their snarls echoing around the room. Others joined them. Milly flinched when Conall leaped up and pushed one wolf onto the floor, his jaws closing around the other's head.

The air rumbled with the sounds of aggression.

A yelp pierced the air; a dark-furred wolf had grabbed Grey One's neck fur in its teeth. Immediately Aela was there, using her own jaws to separate the two. She seized the dark wolf's own scruff, only letting go when he whined. He crouched low and rolled over, belly exposed. Aela bent her neck and he licked her muzzle submissively.

Milly wrapped her arms around her knees, watching as the wolves gradually settled down. She could feel herself trembling, yet it was if someone had wrapped a gauzy blanket around her as an assurance that she wouldn't be hurt. She remained completely still; the blanket stayed in place and the wolves paid no attention to her.

The beams of light from the windows gradually travelled across the floor. As they did, Milly found herself recognising each wolf by the patterns and colours of their fur. It was a much longer stay in the room this time, but when the door opened to release her, she felt no relief - just a strange sensation of peace.

***

Sami looked down at her T-shirt. There was a faint dusting of white flour close to the bottom edge; Sami checked her hands and fingers to make sure they were perfectly clean before brushing the flour away. Why had she chosen to wear the dark purple one to visit Leo?

The correction facility was the only grey building in Redcross. Sami was confronted by a high wall, with an iron-bar gate blocking her way to the main building. On either side of the gate stood a Watchman, their hands behind their backs. Neither of them paid Sami any attention.

She knew the exercise yard would not be outside the facility itself. Whoever built it wasn't stupid.

Sami walked right up to the gate and looked expectantly at one of the Watchmen. "I'm here to visit Leo da Lange."

He raised an eyebrow. "Are you expected?"

"Yes."

"All right, we'll verify that. Follow me." He led her across the small yard and towards the facility. It was a square building that seemed strangely flat, as if it had been partially built and then the builders decided to give up.

The Watchman banged with his fist on the black wooden door. Sami shuddered as she heard the scraping sound of at least two bolts being drawn back before the door opened. A woman in a grey uniform regarded her with indifference.

"She's here to see da Lange," the Watchman said. "Oh."

The guard held up a thin wooden board and ran her gaze down it. "You're Samara Morel?"

Sami nodded.

"Since this is your first visit, we're going to lay down some rules for you and da Lange. He's asked if your visits can be spent inside the library. Follow me."

Sami walked behind her, taking in everything she could. They passed tables and chairs surrounded by wire mesh; presumably, this was where Avrel *used* to visit Leo. Nearby was a large metal door leading to a large space right in the middle of the facility.

"That's the exercise area," the guard announced. "They get an hour of exercise every day. You understand why you won't be meeting da Lange there."

"Is it always this cold?" Sami asked, trying not to rub her arms.

"You get used to it. Anyway, we can only afford to heat the rooms, not the corridors. So how long have you known da Lange?"

"Two years. I'm friends with his sister; we were on the migration together."

"You're not *his* friend?" the guard asked.

"I am. In a way."

The guard nodded. "I get it. Some of our inmates don't get visits at all; from what we overheard, Avrel's pretty upset she's the only person who bothers to visit da Lange. While we're here, she knows me by my first name: Moira. Since you're probably going to be a regular visitor if you behave yourself, you can do the same."

"Thank you, Moira. You can call me Samara."

Moira led her up a short flight of steps and along the landing. Right at the end was a pair of wooden doors; Moira pushed one of them open and called out: "Da Lange? Your guest's here."

Sami breathed in the scent of old books and for one moment she stood in her family's reading room, shelves and shelves of history, legends and stories waiting for her.

Then the guard spoke, and Sami was back in the facility library, with small bookcases around the edge and brown leather chairs set right in the middle, carefully arranged around a square table. The library walls were painted white instead of grey. The books themselves were bound in shades of deep crimson, brown, purple, green and blue, with gold and silver words on the spines. They were an explosion of beauty against the white bookshelves.

Leo sat on one of the chairs. Sami wasn't sure why she was surprised not to find him in a uniform of some kind. Instead, he was in the same clothes he'd worn the day Sami first met him: black T-shirt, blue jeans, dirty brown shoes. His hair was a little longer than when she'd last seen him.

"Hey, Sami," he said.

"Hi, Leo," she replied.

"Here are the rules," Moira announced. "One, and this is the big one: stay in the library at all times. Two: if you're going to keep visiting, the door stays open unless you prove we can trust you. Both of you."

"That sounds fair to me," Sami remarked. She didn't feel quite so cold now.

"Word of warning," Moira's voice was intended to make the listeners' spines chill. "Any funny business and I'll make sure you don't get *any* visitors in the future. That includes this pretty little thing and your sister. Got it, da Lange?"

"Absolutely," Leo said firmly. "No way am I going to mess this up."

"See you don't. I'll let you know when your time's up,

Samara." Moira left the library, leaving the door open.
Leo winked at Sami. *She's got someone standing outside,* he mouthed.

"So," Sami drawled, trailing a finger across the nearest shelf of books, "do you mind if I just choose something and sit down?"

"Nah," he said. "I don't choose anything specific when they put me in here. I just like taking random books and opening them in the middle. It's more fun that way. Besides, it passes the time until the art tutor gets here."

"You have an art tutor?"

"She used to be an actual artist. Now she's teaching us how to draw and paint. I think it's kind of sad: she's painted at least three pictures of Wolf-Lords and now she's being paid to teach people like us basic skills."

"You don't need that, Leo." Sami pulled out a blue book with silver lettering and sat on the chair opposite Leo's. "I've seen some of the things you've drawn. You're really good." She knew that was an understatement. Leo was particularly skilled at drawing things from memory.

"I'm not bad at outlining; she said I've still got to work on the colours and shading. And I really think I'm getting better. Too bad they only let us have one sheet of paper a day in our rooms." Leo smiled, but there was a sadness in his eyes that his normally bright grin couldn't conceal.

"Have you read this?" Sami held out the book to him. "About four or five pages."

"And were those four or five pages any good?"

Leo grinned. "Why don't you find out?"

Sami sat back and opened the book.

Nobody is certain exactly who became the first Wolf-Lord. One story says it was a woman called Annie, who helped a she-wolf raise her cubs. Another says it was a man called Fergus, who faced down a male wolf, the leader of his pack, and remained unharmed. The third story - which is the one most known by the people of Fearainn - is the tale of Elspeth, a young girl of thirteen who raised a wolf cub until it was an adult and then released it back into the forest. Two days later, Elspeth disappeared. The villagers, led by her terrified parents, went in search of her and found her sitting in the middle of a pack of wolves.

All these tales are true. What people cannot decide is which one came first.

***

"Relax, Milly," Frankie said when Milly looked for the eleventh time towards Layden's door. "He's not coming."

Frankie was right. If Barton was going to send a Watchman to collect Milly again, he would have done it by now.

Earlier that day, Milly told Avrel, Sami and Frankie about her encounter with Alasdair and Conall, and about the first feeding session.

"Why would Alasdair want you to take care of the wolves?" Avrel asked.

"You think they deliberately asked for me?"

"Well, yeah, it does look like that. If I'd taken my shift and not gone to see Leo, what are the odds they would have got me to do it?"

Avrel's words followed Milly around well into the afternoon. They drifted through her mind while she tried to concentrate on the tasks Carlene gave her.

This was crazy. She knew it was, so why couldn't she shake the feeling something was catching up with her?

Milly hadn't told her parents about the encounter, or about 'feeding time'.

A stifled yelp caused her to spin around sharply. Frankie had flattened herself against the kitchen wall, her eyes wide with shock.

"What is it?" Milly whispered.

Frankie jabbed a finger towards the main area and mouthed a single word. *That.*

Milly peered around the doorway, expecting to see a Wolf-Lord. Instead, she saw a man of medium height with a trim but powerful build standing just in front of the door, hands on his hips, eyes roving over the tables. His hair was as long, straight and black as Sami's. Milly had never seen a man with hair like that before.

"Good afternoon!" Carlene approached the man and stood just in front of him, blocking him from Milly's view. "Deciding where to sit?"

56

"Afraid not. This isn't a social visit."

"What's wrong?" Milly whispered to Frankie.

"Remember me telling you only two people called me 'Francesca', and one of them's my mum?" Frankie motioned sharply with her head. "That's the other one. Do *not* let him see me."

"Who is he?"

"He's the police chief from my island."

"What's he...oh, I know what's he's doing here. He's Trevel's stand-in. The Watchman from yesterday told me she recommended someone from the Gull Islands."

"Why would she pick *him* of all people?"

"Milly?" Carlene called. "Can you come out here, please?"

Milly did as she was told. "Do they want me to feed the wolves again?" she asked.

The new head of security shook his head. "No. You're wanted at the Complex, but it isn't about that." His dark, shrewd eyes turned to look in one corner of the café, as if searching for something hidden in the shadows.

"What do they want?" Milly heard her voice tremble.

"If it's about what I think it is, you don't want to keep Barton waiting."

Chapter 6

"There you are, Miss Costello," Barton said as soon as he saw Milly. "Thank you for fetching her, Nicholas. Could you wait outside?"

Nicholas nodded to him, then to Milly, and left the office.

"Please have a seat." Barton gestured to the chair in front of his desk. Milly pulled it out and grasped the arms, feeling her wrists tremble as she lowered herself onto the soft seat. Barton was nowhere near as imposing as Weatherhill and Andras, but he had a way of smiling that gave Milly the impression he wasn't smiling at all but looking at the world through a mask.

"I imagine you're wondering why I wanted to talk to you."

Milly nodded. She didn't trust herself to speak.

"First of all, I'd like to congratulate you on doing an excellent job with the wolves. I've been told you handled things very well." When Milly smiled shakily at him, he continued: "Andras was a little uncertain about you, so well done for proving him wrong."

He exhaled through his nose and folded his hands together on his desk. "Let me tell you what this was really all about."

Milly clutched the seat's wooden ridges until they started to hurt her hands.

"During the broadcast earlier this week, I mentioned I made a deal with the Wolf-Lords. There's no need to look so terrified, Miss Costello, you're going to be just fine. The deal was they take someone back with them to experience life their way for a while. Now that could be any length of time - a year, six months, they didn't say. Call it a cultural exchange."

He smiled at her.

"When I was feeding the wolves..."

"They wanted to see if the wolves would accept you and from the looks of things, they have. Aela's given her approval; it's her opinion that really matters in this situation."

"But what if she hadn't approved?" Milly asked. Her voice was far too quiet, but it was the only way she could stop herself from shouting the words.

Barton laughed. "Do you honestly believe you would have been left alone with wolves if there was the slightest chance that they would hurt you? There were at least two Wolf- Lords watching from the balcony all along. You were perfectly safe. They haven't decided how long you'll be with them. Now if the wolves hadn't taken to you, they'd have chosen someone else, but since they seem to like you..."

Milly wanted to scream. Didn't she have a choice in this? But fear tightened around her throat like a noose and she couldn't say anything. Live with Wolf-Lords? For six months?

Was this revenge?

"...so that gives you this evening to pack and get yourself sorted before you leave in the morning. That'll be warm clothes, strong shoes if you have them. Can you do that?"

Milly felt herself nod and heard herself thanking the Premier. She got up and left the office, barely acknowledging the click of the door behind her. Her mind felt foggy. Her whole body was weightless. Her breath echoed in her ears like a frightened bird's cries.

"Hey." That was Nicholas' voice. "Are you all right?"

Milly nodded, willing the fog to clear. She tried to speak, but nothing came out. Hands landed on her shoulders and guided her towards a chair by the wall, firmly pushing her down into it and pressing onto her back until she was staring at the wooden floor. Gradually the fog disappeared, and she was able to breathe.

"I'll walk you back home. You'll need to talk to your parents about..."

"No!" Milly remembered where she was and spoke in a quieter voice. "No, I need to get back to Layden's. Please."

"All right. If you're sure. But you're going to stay here until you don't look like you're about to faint."

***

"Wait, wait, wait." Avrel held up her hands, eyes closed

while she waited for Milly's words to sink it. She opened them again and said: "They want you to go back with them? Back to their home?"

"Yes."

The girls and Carlene were sitting around a table, small cups of tea in front of them.

"And you said you'd go?"

"I didn't say anything. But Barton made it pretty clear that I have to go with them."

"You don't even get a *choice?*" Frankie cried. "How long are you going to be gone?"

Milly shook her head. Her mind was whirling. She couldn't seem to grasp a single thought. "I don't know. Six months, a year? They can keep me as long as they want - or maybe it'll just be for as long as the other Wolf-Lords stay here."

"You can't go," Frankie said urgently. "Milly, you can't go." She reached out as if to touch Milly's shoulder.

Carlene sighed. "Didn't you hear anything she just said? Barton isn't giving her a chance to say no."

"But why you?" demanded Avrel in frustration. "The Wolf-Lords could have had their pick of anyone in the town. Why do they want *you?*"

This was all Milly's fault. If she'd stayed inside and not gone for a walk, she would never have run into Alasdair and he wouldn't have told Andras about her.

"I don't think it matters who goes," Sami said. "If they want someone to come back with them and experience life in their home for a while, I think *anyone* will do as long as the wolves like them. It's just that the first person the wolves accepted happened to be Milly."

"What if the Wolf-Lords don't like her?" Carlene asked coolly. "That could be a problem if she's going to be staying with them."

"Then I guess I'll have to be invisible. They won't dislike me if they don't notice me."

Frankie's eyes flickered with fear as she looked from one friend to another. "Do you think they know about us?"

"No," Milly replied firmly, shaking her head. "I don't think they do. At least, I really, really hope they don't, so we've got to stay calm. If the wolves didn't like me, the Wolf-Lords might have been suspicious as to *why.*"

"Good point," Avrel said, playing with the end of her ponytail. "When did Barton say you're leaving?"

"Tomorrow morning. I need to go and pack as soon as we close." As Milly finished the sentence, tears stung her eyes and she furiously blinked them back.

What was she going to do?

Then suddenly acceptance came over her. She'd travelled a long distance without complaining, and she'd gone hungry without complaining. She could do it again.

She *would* do it. She would survive this.

It wasn't as if she would never see her friends again, or her family.

"Do you want to go home early?" Carlene's voice was gentle now.

"No. I've spent enough time away from work - and I want to spend as much time with you all as I can before the drums sound."

Sami smiled, her green eyes suspiciously bright.

Frankie's face, normally filled with mischief and laughter, was pale and sad. When Milly looked at Avrel, the other girl nodded twice and gave her a tiny grin.

"We're going to say goodbye to you in the morning, you know," Frankie said flatly. "They aren't going to stop us from doing that."

"That's a girl." Carlene pushed herself away from the table. "Now - who'd like to cook what for supper? Since this is Milly's last meal with us for a bit, let's do something fun."

For the next few hours, Layden's echoed with chatter and laughter as the girls prepared food for the customers and themselves. After a few minutes, the talk wasn't even forced. The girls and Carlene kept the sadness and the fear at bay for as long as they could, choosing to talk about things they'd done a few years ago, before the illness attacked Redcross.

"I'm glad none of you are runners," Carlene said. "I know you're not, because you don't look completely exhausted when you arrive here."

"Yeah, and you'd have to hire someone else if we got caught." Frankie dropped some dirty cutlery into the sink. "You know, I think I'd be a pretty good runner."

"Really?" Avrel asked. "Why?"

"I used to sneak around a lot back home. The thing about living on an island is it's a very tight community and everyone knows what everyone else is doing. OK, there are times when that's a good thing, but it can be hard to keep a secret. My friend Jack invented a game: we'd wait until it was evening or a bit earlier than that, and then we'd try and sneak around without the policeman on duty catching us."

"Didn't your mother ever wonder what you were doing?" asked Carlene.

Frankie opened her mouth - then hesitated, a confused frown appearing on her face. "I don't know. I guess she must have thought we were all right as long as nobody was getting hurt."

"Or she knew what you were doing all along," Sami pointed out.

"If anyone knew we were deliberately *sneaking past the police*, why didn't they stop us?"

Milly thought maybe it was because Frankie, Jack and the other island children weren't doing any harm but didn't say it aloud.

"Jack was the best at the game," Frankie said, her smile lighting up her eyes. "He *never* got caught - not ever. All right, I didn't either, but he crept around a lot more than I did. He was the one who called the game 'scaredy-cats'. It was always more fun in the evenings; that way, we didn't know where the policeman was."

"Jack sounds like a lot of fun." Avrel took some clean plates out of the cupboard, careful not to carry too many. "You have no idea. He would get on so well with Leo!"

"My friend Ivy was just like that," Carlene mused. "She was always the troublemaker out of the two of us."

"My sisters and I were the good ones in Kindainn," Milly said. "We wouldn't have done anything like that. Rachel might, just to see if she could; once, she said we were so good nobody ever thought we were capable of being bad."

"Yeah, that sounds like you." Frankie tossed Milly a dishtowel. Milly barely managed to catch it, sending both girls into giggles. "Face it, you're terrible at being bad."

"Grandmother threatened to skin me alive if I even *thought* about misbehaving," Sami said.

"Did it work?" Frankie asked cheekily.

Sami just smirked at her.

"I wouldn't dare run," Avrel admitted flatly. "Not after what happened to Leo."

There were a few seconds of awkward silence, which were broken by Sami. She looked thoughtful. "You know, if I ever tried running, it wouldn't be to see if I could get away with it. Breaking the rules simply because you can isn't a good reason to get arrested."

"What is a good reason?" Milly asked.

"All I know is, if I were to risk spending time in the facility, it would be for something more important. For instance, if one of you was ill and I had supplies but couldn't get them to you before curfew."

"You'd do that for us?" Frankie asked softly. "Yes."

"We'd all do that for each other," Milly said. "It's just none of us have ever actually said that before."

Outside, the drums began to rattle. Carlene sighed heavily. "You'd better go, girls." She took hold of Milly's shoulders and drew her into a quick hug. "Take care of yourself."

"I will."

Outside the café, the drumbeats still hammered away at the evening air. Milly lingered close to her friends, wishing she didn't have to start the walk home. "See you tomorrow?"

"We'll be there," Sami promised.

**

When the emigrants arrived at Redcross, they were led to the Complex and welcomed personally by Premier Barton. Someone had set up tables, on which were arranged a variety of clothes which Barton said were donations by the people of the city.

Everyone knew where the clothes had really come from.

Milly was deeply reluctant to wear things previously belonging to someone who died of the illness. She knew she had no choice. None of them did; the instructions from Barton were to bring just the clothes they would need for the journey.

Now most of the clothes she'd chosen were lying on her bed, waiting to be packed in her knapsack. The only dark item of clothing she possessed was her fleece, which she intended to wear tomorrow morning. The rest of her clothes were in her favourite colours: different shades of pink and blue. She knew the pink shorts were out of the question; it would have to be two pairs of jeans, and at least three T-shirts if she could fit them in. She'd wear a different one in the morning.

Her walking boots were still a comfortable fit, and they were sturdy. She wouldn't have a problem with shoes.

She was in the middle of putting away the unwanted clothes when she saw her pink dress neatly tucked away in the drawer. Milly took it out and held it, studying every inch of the material.

A few months before the Costellos left Kindainn, a travelling market passed through the town; unlike other markets, this one sold cheap but beautiful jewellery that sparkled in the sun, small images painted by artists, carved wooden sculptures and swathes of material as light as cobwebs.

Milly bought some delicate pink material and asked Louise if she would help her make a dress from it. First, they talked about what the dress would look like; Louise told the girl how to cut an outline from the fabric that fit Milly's measurements and gave instructions on how to sew it together, all the while keeping them both supplied with cups of tea, warm biscuits and even warmer conversation.

"It's lovely, Emilia," she said when it was finished, holding it up to the light.

"Is it like the ones you used to make?"

"Almost as pretty...but not quite!" Louise laughed, her eyes twinkling.

If Louise could see Milly now, what would she say?

Milly set her teeth, folded the dress up and put it in her knapsack.

Chapter 7

"You must eat something." Teresa pushed the bowl of porridge across the table to her daughter. "You don't know when your next meal is going to be."

"And if you faint on the walk, they're not going to be very happy with you," Craig pointed out.

Milly stared at the porridge, knowing it would become clay if she tried to take even one spoonful. "I don't feel all that hungry."

"I know you're nervous, but it's going to be fine. Barton wouldn't have made the deal if it wasn't." Teresa held out her hand; after a moment, Milly took it and felt a little courage seep into her at the warmth of her mother's palm.

"If anything does happen," Craig said, "you let us know right away. Don't keep quiet about it."

"Dad, I don't know if I'll be able to..."

"You will. If Barton was able to communicate with Weatherhill and Andras, you can find a way to talk to us."

An idea flickered in Milly's mind like a candle. If she could talk to her parents, she could talk to the girls. She could stay in touch with everyone she loved, even if the messages took days to reach their destination.

Someone knocked on the front door. It was too loud and sharp to belong to Sami, Frankie or Avrel. They couldn't have come for her so soon.

"I didn't say goodbye," she said. "The girls, I - I never said goodbye yesterday, they're coming here..."

"*Calm down*, Milly." Teresa tightened her grip on her daughter's hand. Milly closed her eyes and bowed her head. Bile rose in her throat; she swallowed it down with great effort.

She was so glad she hadn't eaten anything.

"Milly?" Craig had returned. "They're here."

Milly released a shuddering breath. She pushed her chair away from the table, picked up her knapsack from beside a table leg and stood, trying to stop herself from trembling.

Andras stood outside the house, Aela at his side. He gave Milly a brief nod when he saw her. "Are you ready to go?"

Milly nodded back.

Teresa embraced her daughter around the shoulders and kissed her on the cheek. "Stay safe, darling." In a quieter tone, she whispered: "You'll be all right."

"We'll tell the girls for you." Craig squeezed Milly's shoulders firmly once Teresa had released her. "And your sisters."

Milly thought she heard Andras say something to her parents, but she didn't know what it was. As she walked towards him, she looked back towards her parents and saw they understood all the words she couldn't say. All the same, she felt as if a frail cord inside her had snapped, leaving her dazed and uneasy.

The other Wolf-Lords stood at the other end of the street. Milly noticed there were only twelve of them, including Alasdair.

"They know who you are," Andras said as he and Milly drew nearer to them, "and I'm guessing you already know who I am."

"Yes." Milly croaked. She cleared her throat and said much more clearly: "Yes, I do."

"You didn't have a chance to actually meet Gabrielle or anyone else on the way here, but things are different now." Milly could feel his eyes looking down at her. She didn't dare raise hers. "I hope you're not always going to be this quiet. It's going to be a very boring six months if you are."

Six months. Not a year, then. Milly felt her shoulders relax a little.

"That's better."

"Hey! Milly, wait!"

Milly whirled around to see a figure in a blazing red jumper racing down the street. Frankie ran past Milly's house and came to a halt just a few metres away, staring at the figures ahead of her.

"Please," Milly begged, "let me say goodbye to her." When Andras made no move to stop her, she walked back towards her friend as quickly as she could.

"Frankie, I'm so sorry. They got here before you could."

"Good thing I run fast," Frankie panted. She threw her arms around Milly and hugged her tightly.

"Tell Sami and Avrel I'll be back soon. Andras just told

me I'll be gone for six months; it's really not going to be all that long."

"It's going to seem like six years," Frankie complained, "which is why I'm hugging you for all three of us." She released Milly, a deeply worried look on her face. "Look after yourself, OK? If they hurt you in any way, there are going to be a lot of *fur rugs* in the Blue Suite at Layden's."

"He can hear you."

Frankie glared past Milly at Andras. "Good."

Under any other circumstances, Milly would have laughed at her friend's boldness. Not a lot of people would have the courage to even say things like that in the presence of a Wolf-Lord, never mind the hearing of one.

But this wasn't the time for laughter.

"I'll be fine. I promise."

Frankie didn't believe her. Milly could see it in her eyes.

"I *will* be, Frankie." She sighed, not wanting to turn around and knowing she had to. "I have to go."

"See you in six months!" Frankie was blinking rapidly. Her voice was trembling, but she was still smiling. Milly squeezed her hand one last time, let it go and walked back to where Andras and Aela waited.

Andras was staring at Frankie with narrowed eyes, a frown marring his handsome face. As Milly reached him, he turned his attention back to her. "She's from the Gull Islands, isn't she?"

"Yes." Milly was surprised he remembered Frankie at all - but then, Alasdair had remembered her. "She's one of the best friends I've ever had."

As they walked, Milly found her right hand was dangerously close to Aela's head. She managed to curl her fingers away without clenching them into a fist or brushing them against the she-wolf's fur.

"Everyone, this is Emilia," Andras announced, placing a hand on Milly's shoulder. She knew she shouldn't tense, not in front of the Wolf-Lords, but she couldn't help herself. Andras seemed to sense this because he quickly removed his hand. "Emilia, stay close to Alasdair and Sorcha; they're going to be your escorts for the journey."

Sorcha's hair was woven into a messy braid. Her eyes snapped as she grinned, and Milly was reminded of her sister Rachel. Standing beside Sorcha was the black wolf with eyes like embers.

"All right, let's go!"

After a few minutes of walking between her two guards, Milly realised Andras wasn't leading them in the direction of the square or the Complex. They were going towards the outskirts. The houses became smaller and smaller, with paint peeling from the walls and windows that seemed to weep broken glass.

"Where are we going?" one of the Wolf-Lords asked.

"There's a small gate nearby," was Andras' reply. "We'll leave that way. I don't want to make a big exit through the main gate."

Milly hadn't known anything about another gate. She studied the jagged cracks in the ground so that nobody would see her expression. She'd lived in Redcross for two years now; how was it she knew so little about the place?

She already knew the answer. The curfew prevented her and her friends from truly exploring the city.

Although she sensed both human and wolf eyes watching her, Milly kept her gaze focused on the ground and the buildings, determined not to look back.

"I hear you're a cook." Sorcha's voice trilled in the morning air. "Are you?"

"Yes."

"Can you make mushroom soup?" Sorcha asked. "Easily, if I've got the right things."

"Can you tell the difference between a safe mushroom and one that's poisonous?"

Milly shook her head.

"Well," Sorcha said, a gleam in her eye, "that's something we'll have to change."

The gate was small against the red brick of the wall. Andras knocked on it twice and it creaked open from the outside, allowing the travellers to file through one by one into the trees.

***

"I know you don't like it, Avrel, but we need to talk to Jason."

Avrel looked up sharply from her plate of sandwiches.

68

"Why?"

Sami made sure nobody was about to enter Layden's before leaning closer. "Things might go...*wrong* while the Wolf-Lords are here. If that happens, we need a way out. Jason knows Redcross better than all four of us put together."

"What about Milly?" Frankie asked. "She's stuck with the Wolf-Lords for six months. Where's her way out?"

Sami and Avrel glanced at each other, not knowing how to answer. As they did so, Frankie's gaze flickered towards the café door just as Sami's had. Avrel noticed and said: "You can't avoid him forever, Frankie."

"Oh? Watch me."

Sami huffed. "You're going to run into him sometime."

Frankie folded her arms mutinously. "That doesn't mean I can't keep away from him. So where are we going to find Jason? He's not going to want to come in here, not after we were so friendly to him last time."

"Maybe we don't need to go looking for Jason," said Avrel. "I'm not just saying that. What about the library?"

"You mean the facility library?"

Avrel nodded eagerly. "Leo said there are a lot of books about Redcross history there, and some walled cities had - have - hidden passages."

"Even if they do, how many of those passages have been found and bricked off?" Sami wondered out loud.

"The main gate can't be the only way in or out of the city," Frankie said quietly but urgently. "Sami's right - it's a good idea to have a plan, even if the Wolf-Lords don't find out and believe me, that's a *very* big 'if'. There's something I have to tell you."

The door opened.

"Look who's here," Avrel mumbled, eyes sliding away from Frankie. Frankie rolled her eyes, plastered a smile on her face and turned around in her chair.

"Hello," she said.

"I thought you'd be more surprised to see me," Nicholas Ainsley said.

"Sorry to have disappointed you."

Nicholas laughed. "Now *that's* the Francesca I know. Is it too late to get anything for lunch? I need to get something quick before my next shift starts."

69

"We can make a plate for you." Carlene emerged from the kitchen, drying her hands on a clean towel. "I'm afraid we've run out of soup; today's special was very popular."

"Thanks." Nicholas sat down at the table right next to the girls'. "I've heard great things about this place. Can't wait to see if the food's as good as everyone says."

***

"Was that rain?" Sorcha looked up at the grey sky. Beside her, the black wolf did the same.

"I think so." Andras turned sharply to the right and headed into the trees. "We'll stop here; it'll get dark early because of the clouds."

Milly couldn't restrain a sigh as she slipped her knapsack off her shoulders. Although they'd stopped to rest a few times over the day, she was glad they were making camp now instead of later.

That didn't mean she got to rest, though.

"Could you help get some branches and twigs for fires? We need to get them now before it *really* starts raining," a man as grey and grizzled as his wolf said to Milly. "If we don't, we'll be choking on smoke before we even have time to eat. Leave your bag."

There were plenty of broken branches scattered around the bases of the surrounding trees. Milly was forced to snap several in half before she was able to pick them up; before long, her arms were full of so much wood she had to rest her chin on top of the branches to keep them from falling. She noticed one wolf sniffing at her bag before padding away.

She looked around her, trying to see where she was supposed to put the wood. The grizzled Wolf-Lord saw her and pointed at a small earthy space free from rocks, grass or stones. Milly carefully stepped over and deposited the branches right in the middle. There were thirteen people and twelve wolves, which meant there would probably be more than one fire.

As she started collecting branches again, she heard rain pattering on the leaves. She couldn't feel any droplets on her head or running down her neck. Andras had chosen wisely when it came to finding shelter.

"Here." Sorcha was beside her, holding out a small bottle filled with water. "You're going to need this - but don't drink it all at once."

"Thank you." Milly decided not to tell her she'd already been given that advice on the emigration.

Once the fires were lit, she watched as the Wolf-Lords sat or knelt on the blankets spread over the ground, careful not to get too close to the flames. Andras nodded once to Aela; immediately, the she-wolf loped into the trees with the others close behind her.

"They won't be long," Sorcha said. "They can eat what we do, but we don't like our meat raw, so..." She let the words trail off into the air.

Milly's stomach twisted.

"Come on." Alasdair shifted to the left so there was enough space on the red and brown blanket. "You can't eat standing up."

Slowly, cautiously, Milly knelt on the blanket next to him.

"Normally we'd go and find our own food," Alasdair explained. "The wolves help with that a lot. But Barton had his cooks prepare some things for us, so we'll eat those first."

The Wolf-Lords were passing around boxes and taking what looked like dried meat and flatbreads. As she bit into her portion, Milly realised just how hungry she was. The flatbreads had been baked with dried rosemary - one of Joyce's favourite things to cook. Rosemary was one of the easiest herbs to get hold of, and Joyce loved using it in as many recipes as she could.

"Do you know how to make these?" Alasdair asked, holding up a half-eaten flatbread.

"Yes. Well, I always followed instructions, but I have made them at the Complex."

"Could you make them for us?" Sorcha pressed.

"I guess I could, if I had the recipe. I don't think I've baked them enough times to know the recipe by heart. But I could do it."

She glanced over her shoulder to see the hills through the trees. The sky was slowly turning a thick, cloudy blue. It would probably be curfew time soon, yet all she could hear was quiet conversation and the soft crackle of flame.

She got to her feet.

"Where are you going?" Sorcha asked. Milly froze as the eyes of every Wolf-Lord swiftly landed on her.

"I was just...Nothing. I'm sorry." She made as if to sit down again.

"Do you need to walk around for a bit?" That was from Andras.

Milly nodded gratefully.

"Go on. But don't go too far."

"Thank you." She walked towards the edge of the woods and stood there, standing close to the nearest tree. A cool breeze caressed Milly's face and ruffled her hair. It danced around her, carrying the scent of trees, leaves, wet grass and freshly fallen rain.

She closed her eyes and breathed it in.

Chapter 8

Milly awoke to a sound she hadn't heard in the early hours for two years: birds singing. She opened her eyes to see a canopy of green and sunlight above her; the leaves were as beautiful as emeralds with the light shining through them.

Beside her, Sorcha was wrapped in a thick blanket, head pillowed on one arm. Her headcushion was lying to the left; it must have been discarded some time during the night. Milly knew without looking that Sorcha's wolf lay somewhere on her other side.

Aela and the other wolves returned later the previous evening; even though the fires were the only light in the wood by then, Milly was able to see blood staining their muzzles.

Milly sat up slowly, untangling herself from her own blanket. She was surrounded by sleeping figures, both human and wolf, and it didn't seem as if anyone else was awake.

Her shoes were still dry. She shook them in case an insect was inside, slipped her feet into the shoes and manoeuvred her way through the living maze, pausing every so often when a wolf's ears flickered or twitched.

She trod softly on moss and earth, taking care to avoid any twigs or branches lying in her path. Walking on the moss almost felt like walking on a thick carpet. She trailed her fingers across the bark of almost every tree she passed; some were rough and pitted, others smooth with peeling skin. Sunbeams danced between the trees and on tiny flowers emerging from the earth.

It was beautiful.

Eventually, she reached a thick tree with a sapling growing right next to it. Milly sat down between the two trees, wrapped her arms around her knees and gazed up at the sky through the leaves.

Did she have to go back to the Wolf-Lords?

She could stay here. She could live in a place like this, with nothing but trees and birdsong to surround her. Milly tilted her head back and allowed the sun to trickle over her face.

But how would she live? And if she did suddenly decide to leave, she would be making not only the Wolf-Lords unhappy, but Barton as well.

There was a faint rustle to her right. Milly turned to look - and froze, keeping as still as she could. A solitary deer was nibbling at a patch of grass, her dainty ears listening for any hint of danger. Entranced, Milly watched her.

"Emilia!"

That was Alasdair's voice.

The doe raised her head, startled.

"Go on!" Milly whispered, waving her hands at the doe. "Get going!"

The doe looked straight at Milly. Milly clapped her hands; the sound sent birds flitting from branches overhead and frightened the doe into racing into the trees, in the opposite direction the voice had come from. Milly stood up, dusted down the back of her jeans and reluctantly stepped away from the tree.

Conall came bounding towards her. She flinched as the wolf circled her twice, his tail just brushing against her legs. Conall threw back his head and howled to the sky; the sound pierced Milly's lungs like a knife, driving the breath from them.

She took one step in the direction of the camp; immediately, Conall moved to block her. Milly stepped to the right and Conall pressed himself against her legs, growling softly.

"I'm in trouble, aren't I?" she asked.

Conall stared up at her. There was a definite look of reproach in his eyes.

She heard twigs snapping and then Alasdair appeared. He stopped dead when he saw her, his hands flopping to his sides; Milly couldn't tell if his expression was one of annoyance, anger or relief.

"Where were you going?" he demanded as soon as he reached her. "You can't do that. You can't just go wandering off, not in the woods."

"I was perfectly safe!" Milly cried. She clenched her fists, angry that she hadn't considered she might not be safe or the repercussions for disappearing from camp, and that she was being spoken to like a child by someone the exact same age as her.

"We didn't *know* if you were." Alasdair stepped a little closer to her. "Just stay with us, all right? Kendrick says you can't be away from the main group without a guard and if you are..."

"You'll be in trouble as well," Milly finished. Alasdair nodded. "I'm sorry. I didn't think about that."

To make things worse, she'd confirmed she did need an escort by going away from the camp.

Alasdair held out his arm expectantly. After a moment, Milly threaded hers through his and they began to walk back towards the camp, Conall loping alongside them. The other Wolf-Lords were most likely not going to be very happy with her.

As they returned, Milly was greeted with resentful stares. Her insides squirmed, and she tried not to look away from the Wolf-Lords out of sheer embarrassment.

Alasdair squeezed her arm closer to his side. Milly held her head up, strangely comforted by the gesture.

"Now we're all back in the same place," Andras announced, "we can eat."

Sorcha marched up to Milly and stood right in front of her, eyes blazing. "Do that again," she hissed furiously, "and I'll tell Lyall to drag you back."

The black wolf raised its upper lip, revealing gleaming white fangs.

Sorcha whirled around and stalked back to the black jagged remains of the fires, sitting down roughly on the grass. The grizzled Wolf-Lord laid a blanket right next to her with a pointed look; Sorcha obediently shuffled onto it, while the grizzled Wolf-Lord gathered up the husks and ashes to move them aside.

"We won't have a big breakfast," said Alasdair. "It's dried fruit and water, so sorry if you were expecting something hot."

"I don't mind."

"We usually get our own breakfast when we're travelling, but it doesn't look like there are any fruit trees around here. Andras is going to ask for supplies at the next town or city we get to." Alasdair looked down and saw his arm was still threaded through Milly's. "Oh. Sorry." He stepped aside, withdrawing his arm.

"Emilia." Andras stood by one of the fires, his arms folded. He motioned towards the dark blue blanket on the ground at his feet. "Come and sit beside me."

Milly wanted to run away back into the trees, but the look in Aela's silver eyes stopped her from fleeing. She held her head up and walked towards Andras as if he was the Premier himself. She managed to sit on the blanket beside him, all the while forcing herself not to face away from him.

The blanket was surprisingly soft.

As with supper the previous evening, the food was passed around with everyone taking something from a box. It wasn't all that different from supper: a small selection of dried fruit and sweet oat biscuits. The Wolf-Lords also took some of the dried, toughened meat left over from supper and held them out to eager jaws. The grizzled Wolf-Lord picked out a strip of meat from the box and dangled it just above his wolf's head. The wolf leaped up and snatched the food, his teeth narrowly missing the man's fingers; the man laughed raucously and repeated the action with another piece.

Milly watched nervously. She'd seen a dog bite someone who was being too rough with it, and the wolf's teeth looked far sharper than the dog's.

The wolf nudged the Wolf-Lord's arm impatiently and looked at the box, which was still in the man's other hand.

Milly nibbled at her biscuit. The crumbs were dry and caught in her throat; stifling a cough, she quickly unscrewed the top of her water bottle and swallowed. The water soothed her throat instantly. Sighing in relief, she put the bottle down on the blanket with the rest of the biscuit beside it. Ignoring the apple slices she had picked out, she continued to watch everyone as they ate, talked and laughed amongst themselves.

"You should eat."

Milly jumped. Her hand knocked against the bottle, tipping it over and spilling the rest of the water on the blanket. She closed her eyes briefly and opened them to see Alasdair sitting opposite her. He nodded towards the biscuit and fruit, his eyes urgent yet soft.

"We've got a long journey," he said. "And I don't want to patronise you or anything, but you're going to need strength *and* energy." He got up, walked over and held out his water bottle. "Don't worry - I wiped it down."

He smiled at her.

Milly slowly picked up the biscuit.

***

Milly watched the shadows of the clouds pass over the hills. It seemed as if the Wolf-Lords were following the trail set above them at a much slower pace. Even Aela, Conall and the other wolves moved at a gentle pace.

Although she would never have admitted it out loud, Milly knew they were travelling at a slow pace for her benefit. She didn't want to give them yet another reason to resent her, but at the same time she couldn't help but be grateful they'd even thought of that.

She wasn't allowed to dwell on it for long.

"Gabrielle didn't ask me to be part of the escort," Sorcha said. "Alasdair got to go because Conall and Aela are from the same litter, but Lyall was too young. That meant I couldn't go."

"Conall is Aela's brother?"

"You wouldn't know if you saw them side by side, would you? But they are. Gabrielle left Brochan in charge while she was away..." Sorcha gestured towards the grizzled Wolf-Lord, who paced just behind Andras. "...which is probably because he was the one who most wanted her to lead us."

Andras gave her a warning glance.

"Or that's what I was told," Sorcha muttered.

"You said you could show me which mushrooms were poisonous," Milly said after a moment of silence. "Can you really do that?"

"I didn't actually mean you had to make soup for us. You're not here as a cook."

"I know. But you said you would and I'm here to learn and experience things, aren't I?"

Sorcha grinned. "All right. Next time we see a mushroom, I'll tell you if it's poisonous or not *and* how you can tell. Just promise you won't disappear like that again."

"I promise."

"We'll take a rest now," Andras called. "This is a good place."

Sorcha sat down with a loud sigh. Milly knelt beside her, taking care to be on the opposite side as Lyall. She looked at the sky, savouring the combination of a warm sun and a cool breeze.

"Too bad there aren't any deer around," Sorcha mused. "That way we could all have something to eat when we run out of food." When she saw Milly's surprised face, she explained: "Kendrick's only getting supplies from towns and cities so that they can get to know the new *teaghlach* chief; otherwise, we'd be having a roast every night."

Milly couldn't get the doe's soft eyes out of her mind.

"And since Aela likes you so much, Milly, they'll hunt food for you too."

A shadow fell over them. "Sorcha." Both girls looked up to see Andras looming over them, dark against the sky. "Could I talk to Emilia for a moment?"

"Sure!" Sorcha scampered to her feet and moved away with Lyall, leaving Milly alone on the grass, still in Andras' shadow.

"You look confused," Andras said. "What's bothering you?"

"Why did you ask her if you could talk to me instead of just..." Even as Milly said the words, she realised it hadn't really been a request. Or had it? She wasn't sure.

"Because it was polite," was Andras' reply. "And because you're her charge." He sat directly opposite her; Aela lay down beside him, her front paws only inches away from Milly's knees.

"It's probably best if you stay with Alasdair and Sorcha," he said. "The wolves will recognise you as one of us and the others...they don't want to get attached or friendly too soon, but don't let that worry you. Give them time."

Milly was unsure what to think of that. She didn't like the sound of the Wolf-Lords getting *attached* to her, as if she were an object they would have to give back.

But then, wasn't that exactly what she was?

"I want you to feel comfortable with us, Emilia," Andras said seriously.

"I am."

"No, you're not. What are you afraid of?"

Milly's breath froze in her throat. The wind blew some strands of hair loose and into her eyes, but she couldn't raise a hand to brush them away. She couldn't even move at all. "What do you mean?"

"Is it the wolves? You looked as if you were all right with them in the Complex." There was a tiny frown on Andras' face. He looked as if he wanted to reach out and touch her shoulder but was keeping himself from doing so. "Is it us? If you're afraid of us, you don't..."

"It's nothing," Milly whispered. She raised her voice a little and said: "I'm not scared of anything."

Andras looked at her for a moment in silence. Milly had the feeling he was trying to see right through her, through the thin layers she wrapped around herself to the secret she was hiding beneath.

Eventually, he nodded. "All right," he said solemnly. "If you ever decide to tell me what it is, I'll be waiting."

He stood up and walked towards two of the other Wolf-Lords; they greeted him with warm smiles. Aela got to her feet and padded away after Andras. As soon as they were gone, Milly released a shuddering breath. She knew she should feel relieved he wasn't pressing the matter. Instead, the fear she felt when the Wolf-Lords arrived at Redcross had returned, chilling her arms and face.

Sorcha rejoined her. "Hi. I'm back. What did Kendrick want?"

"Nothing. It wasn't important."

***

"Carlene, can I talk to you?"

"Of course," Carlene said without looking up from the pastry she was making. "What is it?"

"We need to talk to Jason. Do you know where to find him?"

Now Carlene did look up. "*You* want to get in touch with Jason, Avrel? It must be really serious."

"Actually, it is." It took a lot of effort for Avrel to get the words out.

Carlene dusted her hands free of flour and put them on her hips, focusing her gaze on Avrel in a way that reminded the girl of her mother. It wasn't a good comparison. "Can I ask why?"

Avrel remembered her parents' reactions when they heard of Leo's arrest. "We need his...we might need his help if things go wrong."

"Couldn't you ask any of the other runners?"

"No, it's got to be Jason," urged Avrel. "He's the only one we know - and the only one who's good enough."

"Good enough to get past the Wolf-Lords?" Carlene asked. "You've probably noticed, but they're working with the Watchmen now."

"If anyone can avoid the Wolf-Lords *and* the Watchmen, it's Jason." Avrel and Carlene jumped; they hadn't noticed Frankie or Sami approach them.

Carlene nodded. "All right. I don't like this, girls. I really don't. You know how much trouble you'll be in if this goes wrong."

"We do," Sami replied.

"And you're willing to do it anyway?"

"It's just a back-up plan," protested Frankie. "How good is Jason at getting out of the city?"

"I don't know. Jason's a strategist, as you well know, and he should be capable of figuring out a way to leave Redcross sneakily. If he hasn't already!" Avrel saw a tiny, fond smile twitch at the corners of Carlene's mouth. "Is this because of the item you stole from the Wolf-Lords?"

Frankie and Avrel looked at each other uneasily. They'd been waiting for her to come to that conclusion.

"Oh, come on," Carlene scoffed. "Just admit it - you stole something and now you think you have to get out of the city. Not quite sure how you're going to do that if they ever do find out it was you, but you don't need to..."

"I didn't say 'stole'."

"Excuse me?"

Frankie moistened her lips nervously. "I said 'liberated'. Not 'stole'."

"What difference does that make?" Carlene frowned suddenly. She looked from Frankie to Avrel to Sami, then back to Frankie. "What did you do?" A look of real fear came over her face. "Girls, what did you *do?*"

Chapter 9

Two Years Ago

"If you don't want your dumplings, I'll eat them," Frankie said hopefully.

Milly barely heard her. The dumplings were probably cold by now, but she wasn't interested in eating them.

"Are you feeling sick or something?" Avrel asked.

"No." Milly pointed towards a cluster of four figures without making it obvious what she was doing. "It's her."

Frankie peered around Milly to see what she was so captivated by. "That's the girl you were telling us about. The wolf-less Wolf-Lord."

The young woman was about four or five years older than the girls and Leo. Her hair was even longer than Sami's or Avrel's and was contained in a loose and untidy plait. She stared at the crackling flames as if she wanted nothing more than to throw herself into them.

"I don't think she is a Wolf-Lord," Milly whispered to her friends.

"What do you mean?" asked Sami.

"She's got a point." Frankie seemed to have forgotten about Milly's food. "Isn't the whole idea of being a Wolf-Lord that you have...well, a wolf?"

"I think there's a bit more to it than that," Avrel said. "If she's not a Wolf-Lord, what's she doing with them? And why is she on the journey?"

"She's miserable. Look at her." The realisation twisted Milly's heart as she kept her eyes on the girl's face. There was no life in it. Her eyes were like coals without a spark to light them. She was completely indifferent to the conversation going on around her.

Couldn't the Wolf-Lords see it?

Over the next few days, Milly kept an eye out for the young woman. She stayed beside the Wolf-Lords and ate with them, but she only spoke to them when she had to, and she never smiled at all.

Sometimes she noticed Milly watching her. The first few times, Milly looked away quickly and pretended nothing was wrong. Then she started giving her small, tentative smiles.

One time, the stranger even smiled back at her.

Eventually, the travellers found themselves outside an open town; Milly couldn't remember if she had been told its name, or if anyone had said what it was. The town was larger than Kindainn, and it looked cold under the grey sky.

Weatherhill and seven other Wolf-Lords headed towards the town. There wasn't anyone waiting to be escorted to the main party, so Weatherhill must have been intending to gather supplies.

Milly noticed the young woman sitting by herself on a log. The black-haired Wolf- Lord approached her and said something, a familiar black and grey shape by his side; the seated figure shook her head without even looking at him. He nodded and followed Weatherhill and the others.

None of the remaining Wolf-Lords came to join the seated figure.

Suddenly she got to her feet and stalked away into the trees, her feet swishing against the grass. Milly looked around. Nobody was watching. She hurried after the disappearing figure, hoping her absence wouldn't be noticed.

It was only when the travellers were out of sight and they were surrounded by trees that she dared speak.

"Hi."

The young woman looked around, startled. The expression of surprise on her face turned to one of wary suspicion. "It's you."

"Yes," Milly said. "I'm Milly."

"Why are you following me?" the stranger demanded.

"Oh. I..." Milly went bright red as she realised how her actions must be coming across. "I'm sorry."

She backed away and turned to go back to the others.

"No, wait."

Milly stopped.

"My name's Debra."

The sound of laughter reached them through the trees.

Debra tensed sharply, her eyes darting over Milly's shoulder before going back to her face again. "They can't see me talking to you."

82

"Are they back?" Milly asked, suddenly terrified and not sure why.

"No. She said she'd be half an hour, but she wouldn't like it if she saw you with me."

"I don't think anyone saw me." Milly hoped her parents hadn't noticed her leaving the main group; by now, they were used to her spending time with her friends during rests.

"It won't be long before they start looking for me anyway, so what do you want?"

"Nothing. I just wondered..." Milly's voice trailed off and she looked down at the grass. A wet leaf was stuck to her boot, along with a few damp green blades.

"Why I don't have a wolf?"

"Yes."

"I'll tell you why: it's because I'm not a Wolf-Lord," Debra said, folding her arms. "Are you satisfied?"

"But if..."

"Milly!" Teresa called loudly. Milly looked back, then at her new acquaintance. She wanted to finish her question.

"You should go." Debra made a shooing motion with her hand. "They'll come after us and then we'll both be in trouble."

Milly walked away, her fingers tingling with cold - and intrigue. Fortunately, her mother hadn't been worried; nor did she ask questions about where her daughter had been.

The remaining Wolf-Lords didn't even notice Debra was missing.

***

Milly didn't have a chance to speak to Debra for the rest of the day, or most of the next one. But in the evening, just when the clouds were beginning to take on a pink tinge around the rims, Milly saw Debra slip away from the edge of the group and melt into the shadows.

Just before she disappeared, she glanced over her shoulder and deliberately met Milly's eyes.

"I'm just going for a walk," Milly said to her parents.

"We've been walking all day," her father pointed out. "Aren't you exhausted?"

"Yes, but..." Milly tried not to look in the direction

Debra had gone. "I need to be alone for a bit."

Craig sighed loudly. "I don't blame you in the least, but don't go too far and don't be gone for too long. It's getting dark."

Milly wove her way into the woods, avoiding roots and holes in the ground until she found Debra sitting on a fallen log. She was in the shadow of an oak tree, her face just about visible in the dim light.

"Can I join you?" Milly asked.

Debra shrugged in reply. "If you want. I'm not stopping you."

Milly cautiously walked over to her and sat on the log, close enough to be companionable but not overly familiar. She was curious about so many things and uncertain how to ask about them, if it was even her business to ask about them.

"How are you finding the journey?" Debra asked, her tone painfully casual.

"It's fine. I like it. Do you know anything about Redcross?"

"No, and I'm not really interested in it. But you didn't follow me out here so that we could have an ordinary conversation, did you?"

"Do you *want* to have an ordinary conversation?" Milly asked.

"I haven't had one of those for ages."

"So...where are you from?" Milly tried to keep her voice light.

***

"She's from Ardlaig?" asked Avrel. "That's an open town, right? I don't think anyone from there is on the emigration."

Sami glanced over to where Debra sat with the Wolf-Lords, chewing on a strip of dried meat. "When are we going to meet her?"

Frankie's jumper was starting to fray a little at the edge of one sleeve; she took hold of a thread and pulled at it, tugging with pale, thin fingers. "Clearly when everyone's not looking," she said. "That's not going to be easy." A grin spread over her face. "And that is what's going to make it so much fun."

"You think sneaking around is fun?" Avrel's voice was sceptical.

"Back on the island, I was the queen of sneaking around. And yes, it *was* fun. Why do you think we did it in the first place?"

Milly checked nobody was walking past them before she spoke. "I've got an idea: each of you creep off and introduce yourself to Debra over the next few days. She knows what your names are; I told her yesterday."

"I just had a thought. Are you sure *she* wants to meet *us*?" Sami asked. She reached up to brush a leaf from her shoulder.

"I think she's lonely."

"Really?" Sami looked at Debra again. "I think she wants to be alone."

"You can want to spend time with someone and want to be alone at the same time," Avrel protested. "I have that with Leo all the time."

"Is that why he doesn't eat with us? Hey, where is he?" Frankie craned her neck around to look for him. "Oh, there he is - he's with your parents."

"What do you think?" Milly pressed, leaning in closer so only her friends could hear her. "Can we do it without getting the Wolf-Lords' attention?"

"Yes," Sami said bluntly. "If you can do it, we can."

"Know what's bothering me?" Avrel muttered, looking uneasily around as two travellers walked past them. "I know the Wolf-Lords haven't exactly been sociable with us, but Debra said Weatherhill doesn't *want* her talking to anyone. Why is that?"

"And is it just her, or is it all of them?" Sami added.

***

"Do you live in their village?"

"It's called Kilshiel," Debra said, "and yes, I do. There are so many people there hoping to become a Wolf-Lord."

In Fearainn, the only way to become a Wolf-Lord was to be chosen by a wolf cub. Fearainn wolves lived for as long as their humans did; there were some records of wolves that were over eighty years old. Nobody under the age of thirteen had ever been selected by a wolf.

"Didn't you ever want to be one?" Milly asked.

Debra laughed bitterly and shook her head. "No, I don't."

"When did you move from Ardlaig?"

Debra went as still as the air surrounding them. She took a deep breath and closed her eyes, pressing her lips together.

Milly waited in silence. The leaves above them sounded as loud as a river.

"I didn't move." Debra opened her eyes and faced the younger girl. "I was part of a deal."

Milly's eyes and mouth grew wide in horror. "You were what?"

"One day, I came downstairs to find Weatherhill in the living-room with my father. He's the Mayor of Ardlaig, and later he told me he'd made a deal with the Wolf-Lords. He never said what kind of deal, but apparently his word wasn't good enough for Weatherhill so he made a guarantee he'd keep it." She smiled sadly at Milly. "And that was me."

"You're a hostage?"

Debra shrugged. "Not exactly. I'm more of a guest who can't leave. It's been two years and I don't know if they're ever going to let me go home again."

***

"That's horrible!" Sami's voice was quiet, but her tone clearly showed how disgusted she was.

"They're just keeping her?" asked Frankie. "What exactly was so important to the Mayor for him to give away his own daughter?"

"She doesn't know." The whole group fell silent as Weatherhill's wolf stalked past them, tail held high; when it was gone, Milly spoke again. "But she's so unhappy. You don't need to talk to her to see it."

"Talk to who?" The girls jumped. Leo had approached them silently and he stood there, arms folded, looking from face to face.

"Who's unhappy?" he asked curiously.

"Her." Avrel pointed towards Debra, who was once

again sitting among the Wolf-Lords and not speaking to any of them. "Her name's Debra and she's been living with the Wolf-Lords as part of a trade of some kind."

"Wait, a trade?" Leo sat down next to his sister and leaned in closer so that nobody would hear them talking. "Are you serious?"

"I wish we weren't."

It was getting colder as the sun went down. Milly wedged her hands under her arms to warm them up. She couldn't imagine the Mayor of Kindainn using any of her children as a bargaining tool, but then again, Debra hadn't said if Weatherhill wanted her as part of the deal or if her father had been the one to include her.

If Premier Barton was a father, she sincerely hoped he wasn't anything like Debra's.

"It won't be long now!" her own father said cheerfully as they got ready to settle down for the night. Milly was now used to sleeping in her clothes instead of nightwear - and to shaking her shoes out in the morning in case any insects crawled inside them during the night. "A couple more days and we'll have reached Redcross."

He frowned at his daughter. "You don't look happy about that, Milly."

"I am. It's just...I don't want the journey to be over yet."

Craig laughed. "It's been quite an experience, hasn't it?"

That wasn't what Milly was thinking. When the journey ended, Debra would have to go back to Kilshiel with the Wolf-Lords. Milly wasn't sure what kind of life she had there, but it most likely wasn't a pleasant one if she was being kept against her will. Weatherhill clearly didn't care about Debra's happiness, or she would have let her go.

Was the deal truly that important?

Milly lay awake for most of the night, watching the sky through the leaves as the fires died and smoke faded into the darkness.

***

The wolves were restless. Weatherhill and the black-haired

Wolf-Lord kept looking at the sky as it grew darker and darker.

"Oh, great," Frankie moaned as a particularly heavy-looking cloud crawled overhead. "We're going to be caught in a storm."

"You can't know that," said Avrel, brushing a leaf out of her tangled hair.

"I do know. I lived on an island, remember? Islanders can smell a storm coming."

Sami sniffed the air delicately. "I can't smell anything."

"You don't know what to look for," Frankie pointed out.

"A selkan would," Milly said. "They can sense a storm coming on the open sea."

"Then they'd be in trouble because we're not by the sea, are we? We aren't close to any buildings, and we can't turn back to the town we left a few days ago." Frankie glanced at Weatherhill. "I think she's realised that, too."

Weatherhill turned to face the travellers. Everybody stopped walking.

"There's a storm on the way," she announced. As if hearing her words, the wind blew through the branches, urging the clouds to move faster. "We need to move quickly if we're going to find somewhere to take shelter."

She started walking again, faster this time. Milly's knapsack felt heavier on her back than it had before, but she kept up with everyone else.

"What if there is no shelter?" she heard someone ask. "I don't think even an Anvador wild storm's as bad as this looks."

"I've been to Anvador," somebody else replied grimly. "Believe me, a wild storm is a *lot* worse than this is going to be."

Thunder rumbled in the distance. Weatherhill made sure to lead everyone under tall trees with thick canopies of leaves overhead, but as the thunder drew closer, she was forced to order everyone to stop moving. She said it was too dangerous to go any further.

Milly looked around wildly for her parents. She couldn't see them anywhere. Had they fallen behind? No - the Wolf-Lords wouldn't let anyone be left behind. Weatherhill had said she wasn't going to tolerate stragglers.

Everyone was putting up shelters under trees, with large branches propping up blankets. The rain that managed to get through the leaves would simply roll off the blankets and onto the ground - unless the rain was so heavy the blankets became waterlogged.

A Wolf-Lord grasped Avrel's shoulders and pushed her towards the nearest shelter; Sami and Frankie hurried after him, their protests dying at the sound of his wolf's growl.

Milly noticed her parents helping another Wolf-Lord tuck some bags under a blanket. She sighed with relief - and then realised someone else was missing. She darted towards the others and huddled under the blanket with them, giving her parents a reassuring nod in the process.

"Debra's not here," she whispered.

"She might be. Maybe she's under another shelter," said Avrel. Just then the first spots of rain began to fall, and the people still out in the open started to move faster. None of the Wolf-Lords had hidden away from the storm yet, but there was still no sign of Debra.

Milly felt cold inside. Something was wrong.

A figure moved between the trees.

"Did you see that?" Sami hissed.

"Where's she going?" Frankie asked. The girls waited for someone to go after the fleeing figure. Milly's heart sank when nobody did.

"Watch my bag."

"Wait." Frankie grabbed Milly's arm urgently. "It's dangerous out there!"

"Which means Debra's in danger. What if nobody sees she's gone until it's too late?"

Reluctantly, Frankie let go of Milly. "I really, really don't like this. And if you get in trouble with Weatherhill or your parents, don't blame us."

"I won't."

Milly ducked out from under the blanket, checked her parents weren't watching and ran away from the camp, hoping no shouts would follow her.

She didn't know where she was going, or where Debra was. All she could see around her were tree trunks and the space between them. "Debra!" she yelled, by now not caring if anyone could hear her. "Debra!"

The only reply was the sound of rainfall.

Milly ran on, her hair slowly growing damper and damper. Water would start soaking through her shoes soon. She'd gone too far away from the camp.

A twig snapped. Milly whirled around to see Debra standing behind her.

"What are you doing here?" she asked. "Don't tell me you were worried about me."

"I was."

Debra laughed, shaking her head.

Milly never knew what made her say the words. They burst out of her mouth. "Come with us instead."

Debra stared at her in shock. "What?"

"You heard me. Come with us. You said you'd been with them for two years; it looks like they're not going to let you go and you don't want to stay with them, do you?"

"I can't go to Redcross! That's the first place they'll look!" Debra was forced to yell as thunder made the trees quiver. "But I'm not going back with them. I can't."

"OK." Milly swiped her hair out of her face. "We'll think of something."

She slid into the camp and joined her friends without anyone noticing. Some of the shelters collapsed during the early minutes of the storm and other travellers were caught in the rain trying to put them up; the fact that Milly and Debra were already wet didn't seem to bother anyone.

Milly saw Debra go over to Weatherhill, who demanded to know where she had been. Debra's only answer was a shrug; Weatherhill marched her over to the nearest shelter and shoved her under the canopy.

"Girls?" Milly said. "I need your help."

***

Now

"What happened?" Carlene asked. The girls had been forced to break off their story in order to serve customers; now, it would only be a few minutes before the warning drums. Plates of food were on the table in front of them, but the girls had barely touched them.

"We stayed at the camp for the rest of the day," said Sami, "and we saved as much food and water as we could."

"I don't even know how we did it." Frankie pressed her palms to the table, shaking her head in amazement. "Somehow, we managed to give Debra the supplies when it was dark and that's when the second storm broke. And because Weatherhill made us travel quickly to make up for lost time, she didn't realise Debra was missing until the afternoon."

"She sent two Wolf-Lords after Debra and the rest of them brought us here," Avrel finished.

"But they haven't come after you, have they? If those two did manage to find her, she clearly didn't tell them and if they didn't, they still won't know about you. You've got nothing to be scared of."

"Actually..." Frankie began, then stopped.

"Actually what?" Sami's voice was soft, deadly and fearful.

"You know when we were talking about contacting Jason and I said there was something I wanted to tell you? Debra's in Redcross. She arrived two days before the Wolf-Lords did."

"She's *here*?" cried Sami.

"How come you never said anything?" Avrel shrieked.

"I'm sorry! I didn't know how to tell you without freaking you out even further or scaring Milly before she left."

"What are we going to do?" Sami was even paler than usual; the lights in the café made her eyes seem unnaturally bright, as if they were filled with tears.

"What we did the first time," Avrel said reluctantly. "Get Debra out. And ourselves if we have to."

"But what about Milly? If things go wrong, she's going to be in more trouble than we are."

"Then we find some way of warning her," declared Frankie. "Eight Wolf-Lords are still in the city. Debra's too scared to come out of the house she's in during the day, so it's got to be at night."

"If it's at night, you've got to deal with the Wolf-Lords *and* the Watchmen," Carlene reminded them.

"That's why we need Jason - if he'll help us. He knows how to avoid the Watchmen and he knows what the city's like at night. He's not an idiot; he's reckless, but he's not stupid."

"What if they've caught him already?" asked Sami. "What if he went running and the Wolf-Lords captured him?"

Everyone fell silent. That was a real possibility.

"I don't know," Avrel eventually admitted. "But we need to watch out for him."

"If he passes by the door, I'll call him inside," said Carlene. She exhaled loudly. "I hope this works, for all your sakes."

Chapter 10

Milly's leg muscles were finally used to walking again. She knew it was going to be a fair distance between Redcross and Kilshiel. Sami must have lived close to Kilshiel, as her town was the first place Weatherhill stopped at on the emigration.

Sami never said where she came from. Milly never thought to ask her.

But she could ask Sorcha and Alasdair. "What was the first place you collected travellers from?"

"Fallyne," Sorcha replied. "Gabrielle said it's the smallest and prettiest city in Fearainn."

Milly couldn't imagine Weatherhill calling anything or anyone pretty.

"Wasn't that black-haired girl from Fallyne?"

Milly barely stopped herself from tensing at Alasdair's question. "She was."

This was not good. If the Wolf-Lords recognised Sami, Frankie and Milly herself, what else did they know about?

Had they seen the girls talking to Debra? Did they know about everything?

Conall made a strange noise in his throat. He looked up at Milly sharply.

Alasdair ran a hand down Conall's head, frowning. "Are you all right?" he asked Milly.

"Yes. I just didn't think you'd remember us."

"Why wouldn't we remember you? We travelled with you from our village to Redcross; it's hard to forget someone when you've walked with them for a long while."

"Not even if you never speak to them?" Milly asked, looking him in the eye for the first time that day.

Sorcha yelped suddenly as she collided with the back of the Wolf-Lord in front of her. It was Brochan; his wolf growled, and Sorcha rapidly took two steps back, holding her hands up. "Sorry."

Lyall, Sorcha's wolf, tucked her tail between her legs, whimpering. Satisfied, Brochan and his wolf turned their backs to Sorcha and Lyall. The whole *teaghlach* had come to a halt, but Conall, Lyall and the other wolves were restless, their ears pricked, their eyes alert.

"What's going on?" Milly asked. "Why have we stopped?"

Before them lay a vast sprawl of trees. A thick mass of shadows loomed between the trunks; Milly could barely see beyond the edge of the wood.

Andras beckoned to a woman, who stepped away from the main group. He spoke to her intently; she nodded once and headed towards the wood, a slim dark shape beside her.

"We can't go any further. All right, we can," Sorcha said, "but we'd be risking a lot because Malnaig is Groves' village and we're just outside his land."

"Whose land?" Milly asked.

"The Groves Wolf-Lords live around here," Alasdair explained. "We're going to ask if we can pass through or not."

Groves must have refused passage on the way to Redcross. "Is that why you took the long way when you were escorting us?"

"Not exactly. They didn't say no because Gabrielle didn't ask. There was no way she was *going* to ask if we could pass through - Matthias Groves wasn't exactly a friend of hers."

"She hated him," Sorcha added helpfully. "But he might let us through now Kendrick's in charge."

"They did not hate each other. They just...didn't like each other much."

All they had to do now was wait for Groves' reply. For the first time on the journey, Milly found herself fighting boredom as everyone stood outside the trees. She wondered if she should be feeling nervous instead, and why that wasn't the case.

"You'll love Kilshiel." Sorcha nudged Milly, smiling broadly. "It's small, but it's home and we wouldn't have it any other way."

"I guess I'll find out what it's like when we get there."

"It'll be your home, too," Alasdair reminded her. Milly was struck by the warmth and reassurance in his voice. "I hope you'll think of it like that while you're with us."

"I hope I will too." Secretly, Milly hoped she didn't. If she thought of Kilshiel as home, she wouldn't want to leave any more than she had Kindainn and she *had* to get away.

She couldn't get agitated, so she smiled.

"How close is Malnaig to here?" Milly asked, peering around Brochan's bulky shape

"Not far. The Groves wolves probably already know she's there," Alasdair told Milly. "Wolves can sense intruders in their territory."

"I hope they'll be friendly," Sorcha moaned. "And I hope Elsie doesn't have to wait for Groves for long. If she comes back with a 'no', we're going to have a very long journey." She pushed away Lyall's nose from her waist. "There's also another problem."

"What is it?" Milly asked.

"You know about Joshua Haigan, right?"

"Of course."

"He's Matthias' ancestor. This was Haigan's land."

Just then Elsie jogged out from under the trees, her wolf beside her. When they reached the main group, they stopped dead and faced Andras, who looked at Elsie questioningly.

"He's waiting for us."

"Is that a yes?" Andras pressed.

"I couldn't tell. All he said was that he wants to speak with you."

"Are he and Finella alone?"

Elsie shook her head. "Ten others, and their wolves."

"Is that good or bad?" Milly whispered to Alasdair.

"I don't know." Alasdair sounded very worried. "From what I've heard of Matthias, it could be either. But I'd think he was an idiot if he and Finella had come alone."

Andras and Aela started moving towards the dark mass of trees. The others followed without needing to be told. It didn't take them long to find the Groves Wolf-Lords, who stood just in front of a fallen tree that was propped up by a large rock.

Although Matthias Groves was wearing a loose grey shirt, dusty black trousers and boots, his silver hair made him appear more dignified than Barton had ever looked. His blue eyes watched as the Andras Wolf-Lords approached. Beside him stood a white wolf, who regarded Aela with glowing amber eyes.

Milly guessed this was Finella.

Behind them, ten other Wolf-Lords and their wolf partners waited in silence.

"Kendrick," Groves said, inclining his head slightly. His voice was quiet and solemn, but it carried through the trees loudly enough for everyone to hear.

"Matthias." Andras inclined his head in return. "I would like to ask permission for myself and my *teaghlach* to pass through your land."

"You could have passed through two years ago," Groves said. "Gabrielle and I had our differences, but I wouldn't have allowed that to affect basic friendliness or courtesy."

"Will you let us pass now?" Andras asked.

Beside Milly, Sorcha held her breath.

"Of course. In fact, I'd like to invite you to eat with us tonight."

Groves' eyes fell on Milly. She held his gaze despite the chills running down her arms.

Finella stepped towards Aela and sniffed noses with her. The she-wolves made Milly think of two queens greeting each other - one clad in snow, the other in shadows.

Groves looked back towards the twenty figures. "Tell his Lordship to start making preparations."

One of the pairs detached from the group and raced into the distance, branches snapping loudly beneath their feet.

Andras and Groves headed deeper into the trees, side by side.

***

Milly emerged from the trees to see Malnaig spread out before her. She saw houses made from brown and grey stone; all of them were topped with thatched roofs. This village was probably even older than Kindainn; like Kindainn, Malnaig was filled with laughter. Wolves walked among the buildings as naturally as cats or dogs would.

"You're welcome to get cleaned up," she heard Groves say to Andras. "I know you've been walking for a while; if you wait a bit longer, there'll be heated baths ready for you."

"Thank you." Andras' voice was quiet. "It'll be good to get clean in warm water." Most of his Wolf-Lords laughed softly and Milly found herself biting back a smile. Heated water would be such a relief.

A short while later, she was alone in a small room with a metal tub in front of her. Steam wafted enticingly from the tub; beside it, she could see two buckets of cold water, just in case the contents of the tub were too hot, and two tiny bottles filled with pale pink liquid.

Milly climbed into the tub and submerged herself completely, allowing the water to seep through her hair. It was like settling into a comfortable bed after a long and cold day and waking up completely refreshed. She washed herself thoroughly, using the water in the buckets to rinse her hair.

Someone knocked on the door. "Excuse me - are you nearly finished? There are others waiting for the tub."

"Yes. Sorry." Milly clambered out of the tub and wrapped herself in a fleecy towel.

"There's going to be a roast tonight, so if you've got any nicer clothes it would be a good idea to wear them. But nobody's going to mind if you don't. Leave your dirty clothes; we'll take care of them."

Milly dried herself quickly and roughly, tousling her hair in the process. It would have to dry naturally. She picked up her bag and hurried into the room she had been allocated, still wrapped in the towel.

Her knapsack was tucked safely beside the bed. Milly made sure the shutters were closed before reaching into the bag and pulling out her dress. It wasn't creased, but Milly hadn't brought her sandals with her.

She opened the bedroom door to see the speaker - a short woman about Teresa's age with brown hair in a bun - picking up the empty buckets. "Can I ask you something? I know you've done a lot for us already, but..."

"What is it?" the woman asked.

Milly held up her dress with one hand. "Does anyone have some spare shoes I could borrow?"

Half an hour later, she was running her fingers along the top of the soft shoes, glad they were her size and that someone was willing to lend them to her. They were made from soft material, and they were warmer than her

97

sandals. They went perfectly with her dress.

She could smell smoke and roasting meat through the gap in the window shutters. The scent was rich and made her mouth water. Laughter echoed through the stone walls.

Her mother's cooking smelled of home. When she and her friends cooked and baked, the only smells they had to watch out for were burning, and freshly baked bread and cake.

Milly would always associate roasts with sunsets and warmth on cold evenings.

She checked the ends of her hair. They were just about dry enough. She took a deep breath, stood up, smoothed the dress down and walked out of the house.

The sky was fading from blue to dusky rose, forcing the buildings to cast long, thick shadows. Wolves and humans walked past the house, all headed in the same direction. Milly watched as a child walked a little too close to a Groves wolf, only for his mother to grab his shoulder and quickly steer him away.

She wondered if she should wait for Alasdair or Sorcha - but since everyone was going to the same place, she thought she might as well meet up with them there. She joined the walk and soon found herself in what she thought must be the village square.

Right in the middle of it were three large fires, each with a hog turning on a spit above it. Men turned the spits, their hands safe inside thick gloves; others carved slices of dripping meat and put them on plates, handing them over to waiting hands and the jaws of hungry wolves. In the background stood a large stone building with open doors leaking warm, golden light. People sat on benches or walked around while eating; Milly saw them smile and laugh, and suddenly she longed for her friends with a desperation that made her throat ache.

"And this is her?"

Groves' voice came from somewhere to her left. She turned to see him approach, Andras beside him; Aela walked on Andras' right, Finella on Groves' left. Andras had changed into a smarter but comfortable-looking T-shirt that made Milly feel slightly overdressed.

No. She loved her dress, and she loved wearing it. She

wasn't going to be ashamed of that.

"Emilia, I want you to meet Matthias Groves," Andras said formally. "Matthias, this is Emilia Costello."

"It's a pleasure." Matthias held out a hand; his grip was firm, warm and calloused. "So you're the new guest of the Andras Wolf-Lords."

"I am." Milly wasn't sure if she was supposed to curtsey or not. How did you address the leader of a Wolf-Lord *teaghlach*?

"Aren't you cold in that dress?"

"A little," Milly admitted, "but I don't mind."

"Well, if it gets too much for you, go inside there." Matthias gestured towards the open doors. "Percy!"

A young man came over to join them. He was wearing baggy blue jeans and his hands were jammed in the pockets of his dark grey fleece. He had curly dark blond hair that was almost brown, and there was a faint dusting of a beard on his chin and around his mouth. He was perhaps twenty years old and deeply handsome; the smile he gave Milly made her think of Leo and Jason.

"Everything's going brilliantly," Matthias said to him. "Thank you!"

Milly frowned. Where was he from? She didn't recognise that accent.

"Perhaps Percy and Brynn could be Emilia's escorts for the evening?" Matthias looked at Andras as he spoke.

Andras hesitated a moment, then nodded.

"I wouldn't mind that. Come on and we'll get some food." Percy led Milly towards the nearest spit. "This is the second roast we've had in two months; I'll have to ask Matthias if we can have guests more often."

"Who were the guests the last time?"

"There weren't any guests. We were celebrating my engagement. I proposed to Brynn and she told me to ask Matthias' permission; in fact, I should have done that first, but he didn't mind."

"Is she a Wolf-Lord?" Milly asked, wondering if Brynn might be Matthias' daughter.

"No, but it's still tradition to ask the leader before the girl."

"Congratulations on your engagement," Milly said politely.

99

"Thank you."

By now, they had reached the spit. "You go first," Percy said, making a surprisingly elegant motion with his right arm.

"There you go," the carver said, holding out a plate filled with meat. "That enough for you?"

Milly nodded and took it. "Thank you."

"Want the same, your Lordship, or a bit more?"

"I'd like a bit more, please." Percy waited for the carver to finish preparing his plate. "How old are you, Emilia?" he asked.

"I'm seventeen."

Percy nodded and smiled. "I thought you were about that age. I have a sister a bit younger than you."

"Is she here?" Milly looked around for a girl with the same curly hair and bright grey eyes as Percy.

"No, she's back in Silverdon. I haven't seen her for over a year." He sounded surprised, as if he couldn't believe it had really been that long.

"You're from Anvador?" Anvador was the land closest to Fearainn; it was divided into five regions, each of which was governed by noble families. There was always more than one family in charge of each individual region, which didn't make sense to Milly. It was like having more than one Mayor in a town, or more than one Premier in a city.

"I came here for a visit and fell in love - with more than just the place." Percy shivered as the wind ruffled the nearby flames. "I can't see Brynn anywhere. She might be inside the hall."

They walked into the building, taking care to balance the plates they carried. Inside were more benches and chairs arranged around the edge of the single room. A table was set against one of the walls; two people were scooping ladles full of liquid out of urns and into cups.

Percy spotted a young woman sitting by herself right at the back of the room, facing the open doorway. She raised a hand and waved them over.

"Brynn," Percy said as they reached her, "this is Emilia."

Brynn was petite and pretty, with a dainty foxlike face and light green eyes. A ribbon of a darker green was woven into her hair. She smiled shyly at Milly. "Hi."

"Hi," Milly replied, suddenly shy herself.

"I'll get us all drinks," Percy said. He gestured towards the bench. "Don't wait for me to come back."

Milly and Brynn sat down awkwardly. Milly picked up a piece of meat in one hand and bit into it cautiously. The meat was juicy, tender and steeped with flavour.

"It's good, isn't it?" Brynn said. "We only have hog roasts when we're celebrating something, or when we've got important guests."

Milly studied Brynn's neck, wrist and fingers closely, but couldn't see a braided band of three colours, the normal sign of engagement in Fearainn. She devoured the rest of the piece and turned her attention to the next, taking care not to drip any grease. If she got any on her dress, the stain would never come out.

When Percy returned, he was carrying three cups.

Steam wafted up from them into the air. "I think you'll like this. It's a warm spiced apple drink." He placed one on the bench next to Milly before sitting next to Brynn. Milly sipped at the drink and tasted winter nights.

She saw a familiar red and grey shape enter the building, Alasdair just behind him. Alasdair's eyes met hers and his eyebrows rose in a tentative question, his eyes darting to the space on the bench beside Milly.

"Is it all right if Alasdair joins us?" Milly asked Percy and Brynn.

"Who?" Percy spotted Alasdair and Conall. "Is he your assigned bodyguard?"

"One of them. Alasdair, this is Percy and Brynn." Milly's plate was empty, so she quickly picked up her drink to make more room.

"Hi," Alasdair said as he sat down next to her. He was wearing a red shirt a few shades lighter than Frankie's jumper; Milly wondered if he'd brought it himself or if it was borrowed, like the shoes she wore.

She didn't remember Alasdair because she hadn't cared to notice him.

Conall looked at the plates with gleaming eyes.

"No, you've had your share," Alasdair said reproachfully. "I'll get you more in a minute, OK?" But he was smiling as he said the words. As he smiled, he turned to look at Milly and his hazel eyes seemed almost golden.

101

Chapter 11

"What delectable sweets were available in Layden's Café over the past few days?" Leo asked as soon as he and Sami were inside the library. "Cakes. Pies. That kind of thing."

"Chocolate cake, plain scones, apple and cinnamon cake...oh, and Carlene wants Frankie to make strawberry tarts first chance she gets."

Leo groaned. "I wish I hadn't asked now."

"What sweets do you get here? *Do* you get sweets here?"

"Yeah, but compared to Layden's cakes, eating them is like eating paper." Leo glanced at the half-open door, then leaned forward and whispered: "There's one guard who we think eats the best sweets. I kind of started calling him 'Mr Eatsalot' behind his back and now everyone calls him that."

"Does he know?" Sami asked playfully.

"I hope not, or we're in trouble."

Sami browsed the shelves before noticing a purple book with silver lettering. "I know this one - my family used to have a copy. It's one of my mother's favourites."

She sat down on the nearest chair and opened it at the beginning. The book contained a collection of stories and legends from Fearainn, Anvador, Tirmor and Reothadh.

Sami wanted to tell Leo everything that had happened over the past few days, but the door was open and there would be someone outside listening. She couldn't even ask him if Jason was in the facility; if he was, Leo would have seen him during the exercise time. But if she did ask, the listener would want to know why she thought he might be there - and if there was a reason for Jason to be there in the first place.

Instead, she asked: "If you could have any sweet you wanted right now - anything at all - what would you have?"

"Pink sugar ice cream."

Sami raised her eyebrows. Ice cream? That was a rare treat in Redcross - even more than Frankie's strawberry tarts - and pink sugar was even rarer than chocolate. Sami remembered tasting it back in her old house; it made her taste buds tingle.

"I had it once. Never forgot it," Leo said wistfully. "What's your book about?"

Sami told him. "My grandmother used to read the scarier stories to me when I was little." Sami's favourite story had been The Cruel Princess, but her grandmother always refused to read that one.

"Did they scare you?" Leo asked.

"No. Well, one kind of did. It haunted me for ages after I first heard it. It was the Tale of the White Hare. Do you know it?"

"I don't think so." Leo rested his hands on his knees and gazed at Sami. "What happens?"

"Every year, a white hare runs across the hills and..."

"Sorry - the hills of where?"

"I'm not sure," Sami replied. "It could be anywhere except Tirmor. Anyway, every year a group of hunters go after it and they're unsuccessful every time. To make things worse, one of them disappears. They always come back with one hunter missing. Nobody knows what happens to them.

"The main character is a hunter called Elias. One time, the person who disappears is his older brother; Elias blames the hare and decides to go on the hunt the next year to get revenge."

"Uh-oh," Leo mumbled. In the old stories, people who sought revenge very rarely got what they wanted.

"He goes on the hunt, and the group splits up."

"Why did they do that? If one of them disappears every time, why would they want to split up?" Leo asked, frowning.

"I never liked that either. Elias ends up alone - and he sees the hare standing on top of a hill. It looks at him, and he shoots it. That's always the part I hate the most, but it's not the worst part."

"Because Elias becomes the hare, right? The hunter who kills the hare ends up taking its place."

Sami nodded.

Leo shook his head, laughing softly. "Are there any happier stories in that book?"

"Quite a lot." Sami flipped through the yellowing pages; they crinkled softly between her fingers. "Want to hear one?"

For the next hour, she read out loud and the library echoed with ancient tales. Sami knew she couldn't make the stories come alive the way her mother and grandmother had, but she told them as best she could.

After the first three stories, she began to forget where she was and what she needed to do. She was lost in the stories, wandering deeper and deeper with the turn of each page.

"Excuse me."

Sami jumped; she was so close to the end of the book.

Moira stood in the doorway, her arms folded. "Time's up. Sorry to interrupt your story-time, da Lange."

She didn't sound remotely apologetic.

Sami slowly stood up and replaced the book. "I'll be back soon," she said softly. Leo nodded, and said nothing.

The air bit into Sami's hands and face as soon as she was outside. It had been sunny when she walked into the facility; now the sky was an unpleasant grey.

One of the Watchmen stood to the side of the gate, casually gazing over the street. It was the same Watchman who had collected Milly from Layden's. He was in the regular uniform but unlike the others, he wore a red band around his upper right arm. Once Sami saw the red band, she couldn't take her eyes off it. She'd lived in Redcross for two years; why hadn't she seen any Watchmen wearing one of those before?

He noticed her and smiled. Encouraged, she walked over to him, smiling with as much charm as she could. "Hi. I'm Samara Morel; it's nice to meet you."

"Nice to meet you too. I'm Tony Rowe." Sami was so stunned, she couldn't move.

"Tony...*Rowe?*"

"Ah." Tony's smile broadened. It made his hazel eyes twinkle warmly. "Judging from your reaction, I'd say you know my brother."

Until that moment, she had no idea Jason even had a brother. "Yes, I've met Jason. How is he? I haven't seen him for ages."

"He's fine. He's Jason," Tony said, as if that was an explanation for everything.

"Will you tell him we miss him at Layden's?"

"I will. Oh, how's your friend doing? The one Barton

kept asking to feed the wolves? He hasn't fed her *to* them, has he?"

"No. And we think she's all right." Sami nearly said 'hope' instead of 'think'. Why hadn't Milly contacted them yet?

***

"Can I ask you a favour?" Milly said to Percy and Brynn.

"What is it? We'll do the best we can." Percy scraped the remnants of his porridge from the bowl.

"I've got friends and family back in Redcross. I need to send them messages to let them know I'm OK. Would you pass them on for me?"

"We'd be happy to," Brynn said reassuringly. "Thanks."

"Anyone want some more?" a Groves Wolf-Lord asked, putting a pan brimming with porridge down on the table in front of them.

"I will, please," Milly said. Next morning, it would be biscuits and fruit for breakfast. The porridge was like a comforting blanket. "Thank you."

"Brynn? Your Lordship?"

Percy and Brynn shook their heads and the Wolf-Lord moved on to the next people.

"Percy, why do they call you 'your Lordship'?" Milly asked curiously. The words weren't spoken with automatic respect, the way someone said "Yes, Premier" back in Redcross. They sounded friendly, a term of endearment.

"Because that's what I was," Percy said simply.

Milly's eyes grew wide and she nearly fell off her seat. "You were a Lord?"

"Lord Percival Monray was my name in Silverdon. I like being plain Percy much better."

"It suits you more," Brynn said.

Milly wanted to ask why Percy had given up his life as a Lord in Silverdon - and realised he gave her the answer yesterday.

"I know you've only been with them a few days," Percy said quietly, "but you don't have to see your time with Wolf-Lords as a chore."

Milly was trying not to see it that way, but the

105

difference between Percy and herself was Percy had *chosen* to live with Wolf-Lords. But then, her stay was only going to be for six months. His was for life.

He might not even be able to give a ring to Brynn on their wedding day.

"You can enjoy it, if you give it a chance." Percy smiled reassuringly. "You might want to go and write your messages before it's time to leave."

Nearby, Malnaig villagers were placing small packets of supplies into bags, ready for the departure of the Andras Wolf-Lords.

"I don't have any paper. Or pens."

"Ask Keith the cook. He'll help you."

In the kitchen, Milly quickly scribbled two messages, one for her parents and the other for her friends. The one to her friends was almost the same as the one to her family, but there was a hidden sign inside she hoped they would find. She folded the messages carefully and gave them to Percy. The message to the girls was addressed to Layden's.

"Have a safe journey," Percy told her, "and please remember what I said."

"I will." Milly shouldered her knapsack, said goodbye to Percy and Brynn and joined the Andras Wolf-Lords.

"Good luck," Matthias said, shaking Andras' hand. "Travel well."

Andras nodded solemnly. "Thank you for everything, and for your advice."

The two wolf queens moved closer and nudged each other with their muzzles. Then Aela turned around, tail held high and, together with Andras, led the travellers out of Malnaig.

***

"Hey, Frankie, guess what's at the market today. *Strawberries.*"

Frankie's eyes brightened with excitement. "Really?"

"Yup," Carlene said. "Think you can do a batch oy your famous tarts?"

Two months after starting work at Layden's Café,

Frankie asked if she could bake some strawberry tarts. They were deeply loved on her island and - Frankie admitted this to her friends later - baking them would remind her of the people and the place she'd left behind.

The tarts were gone in one day.

"Absolutely - but could I set some aside for us?"

"Oooh." Carlene pursed her lips. "I don't know about that." Her mouth stretched into a grin and she pressed some money into Frankie's hand. "Go on and get the strawberries before they're all sold."

Even if Frankie didn't know where the market was, all she needed to do was follow the crowd. Goods from the market were sold very quickly and Frankie wanted to get as many strawberries as would fill her tiny basket.

When she reached the main square, she headed straight for the stall that was painted dark green. Steph, the vendor, smiled as she saw the girl approach. "Hi, Frankie."

"Hi, Steph. Please tell me you've got some strawberries left."

"I certainly do." Steph held out her hand; Frankie gave her the basket and watched as Steph scooped up the fruit and placed enough in the basket to fill it, but not to overflowing.

"They look good." The strawberries were plump and a beautiful, deep red.

"They *are* good. It's a great crop this time."

Frankie handed over the money Carlene gave her and waited for Steph to count out the correct change. Her gaze roved around the market, over all the people at the different stalls.

Jason Rowe was there, looking at the bread.

"Here you go." Steph gave Frankie a tiny amount of change.

"Thanks, Steph." Frankie shoved the coins into her pocket. "Jason!" she shouted. "Jason!"

He turned around to see who was calling him and beamed when Frankie ran up to him. "Hey, Frankie! What's going on? Do you know how Leo is?"

"I need to talk to you." Frankie grasped Jason's elbow and walked him into a nearby street, where there was nobody about. "To answer your question, Leo's fine. Here's one from me: how many people know your brother's a Watchman?"

Jason flinched and looked at the ground, his hair falling over his eyes. "I don't tell a lot of people about Tony."

"Yeah, we realised that. Is that how you know which Watchman patrol goes where and who's out every night?"

"Tony doesn't know what I'm doing," Jason said quietly. "If he did, there is no way he'd let me get away with it. He'd arrest me himself."

"He's not telling you who's doing what where, is he?"

"No. He leaves the schedules in his bedroom; I go through them when nobody's looking and memorise them." He exhaled loudly and brushed his hair away from his forehead. "I don't even know why I'm telling you this. Tony said you guys *miss me* at Layden's - is that meant to be a code? Last time I was in there, you weren't exactly friendly towards me and I don't blame you."

Frankie was about to suggest he come back with her to Layden's so they could explain everything when she saw that Jason was not looking at her. He was frowning, his gaze focused somewhere over her left shoulder. She turned to see what attracted his attention and her stomach dropped.

A horribly familiar figure stood several metres away from them, his arms folded. When he saw Frankie had noticed him, he began to walk purposefully in their direction.

Frankie turned back to Jason. "Get going. Now." "You know him? Who is he?"

"Trevel's replacement."

Jason went pale. He was about to walk away when Nicholas called out: "No, stay where you are." Frankie and Jason waited until he stood in front of them.

Nicholas wasn't a tall man, but he didn't have to be. He looked at Frankie, sighed through his nose, glanced down at the pavement, then up at Frankie again. His lips were set in a hard line.

"I was really patient back on the island," he said. "I know you and Jack didn't see it that way, but the truth is I let you get away with a lot."

"That's because you couldn't prove it was me."

Nicholas nodded. "You're right. I couldn't. And...well, you caused trouble, but I know you didn't mean harm and you're just as much my responsibility now as you were back then."

"What are you talking about?" Frankie asked. "Since when have you been responsible for me?"

"Yeah, you're not her father," added Jason.

Nicholas didn't even glance at Jason. "As chief of police, it was my job to protect everyone. That included you. That's also my role as head of security, which is why I want you to listen to this."

He turned his attention to Jason. "From now on, you're banned from Layden's."

"What?" Frankie yelled.

"Oh, really?" Jason folded his arms in his best casual but confident pose. "Hate to break it to you, but you don't own Layden's. Carlene does. She's the one who decides who does and doesn't go in, and last time I checked, she didn't have a problem with me eating there. Why don't you take it up with her?"

Frankie shook her head wildly, but it was too late. Nicholas' mouth was already stretched in a grin she knew all too well.

"I'll let Francesca do that for me. If Mrs Layden doesn't get your picture up on her wall of unwanted visitors..."

"She doesn't even *have* one of those," Frankie said.

"...I'll be having a little chat with the Premier."

"Hey, wait just - " Jason began.

"You can't do - " Frankie cried at the same time.

"And if I ever catch you talking to Francesca or any of her friends again," Nicholas said, his voice hardening dangerously, "I'll slam you into the facility so hard they'll be scraping pieces of you off the walls. Come on, Francesca, I'll walk you back."

He put a hand on Frankie's shoulder. Frankie was too stunned to react at first. It was only when they were halfway down the street that she found her voice. She stopped and spun around, jerking her shoulder free.

"Jason's right. You are not my father. And since when do you tell people who they can and can't talk to?" she asked. "That *isn't* your job."

"No, it wasn't," Nicholas agreed. "Not on the island.

109

Turns out I've got a few other duties as Barton's head of security - and that includes telling you to stay away from people like Jason Rowe. He's trouble, Francesca."

"So was Jack," Frankie challenged.

"Jack was a kid. So are you. Jason isn't." Nicholas held Frankie's gaze until she dropped her eyes. "Come on," he said again, gentler this time. "They'll wonder where you are."

Frankie kept a tight hold on the handle of her basket as she walked. She didn't look at Nicholas or speak to him as they turned the corners and headed down the streets that led to Layden's. She knew he could sense she was angry, but she refused to talk to him about why.

"Will you give Carlene the message?" Nicholas asked as soon as the café came into view.

"Yes," she replied, knowing she didn't have a choice in the matter.

"Good." Nicholas nodded at her and set off back the way they'd come. Frankie exhaled, held her head up and walked into the building.

"We've got a problem," she said as soon as she'd put the strawberries away. "I found Jason in the market and..."

"He said no?" Avrel interrupted.

"He might have done if I had the chance to ask him. Because guess who else I ran into."

"Tony?" asked Sami.

"Worse. Nicholas. And he was not happy to see me talking to Jason." Frankie was still shaking a little from the encounter.

"Did he say anything?" Avrel asked nervously.

"Only that Jason is now officially barred from Layden's."

"Oh *no*," groaned Sami. "Can he actually do that?"

"Frankie, please tell us you're not serious!" Avrel protested.

"I am. Jason's not allowed in here, and he's not allowed to talk to us." Nicholas had only said if he *caught* Jason talking to the girls, but both Frankie and Jason knew what he really meant.

"You could ask Leo," Carlene suggested. "He only ran once, I know, but he might remember some of Jason's instructions and the best routes."

"There's just the slight difficulty of an open door and a guard listening to every word," Avrel reminded her.

An even worse thought entered Frankie's mind; she very nearly groaned aloud, like Sami had. "We've got another problem. If Nicholas is watching Jason, he's also watching the other runners, which means we can't risk getting in touch with them either."

"You don't know that."

"*You* don't know Nicholas."

Sami sighed heavily. "We've got no choice. It needs to be Leo. I don't know how but it's got to be him - if he'll help us. Do you know where Debra is, Frankie?"

"Yup. She said she's lodging at Thistleton House."

Carlene raised her eyebrows. "She's managed to get Phoebe Macton to take her in? That's impressive."

"We've got to do this quickly," Avrel said, "because if we don't, they'll find her. And I don't want to know what will happen after that."

Chapter 12

"What colour are the roses in Kindainn?"

"They're mostly pink," Milly said, "all kinds of shades. Magenta, pastel...there was one that had petals with white centres and dusky-pink edges. We had white ones as well, but outside the Mayor's house there were these gorgeous crimson blooms. The Mayor used to say only a Reothadh rose was redder than they were. They made the house stand out even more!"

The Wolf-Lords had stopped for a few hours to take some rest. After sitting still for a while Milly felt herself becoming restless, so she asked Andras if she could explore the area further. The only condition was that Alasdair went with her.

"Did you have a favourite rose?"

"Yes. They were the ones outside our home. They're a lovely pale pink and they look like little frills." Milly imagined running a fingertip along the velvet-soft ridges of the rose petals. "They smelled sweet and light. Like spring."

They would be in bloom at this time. Milly hoped the person living in the house after her family loved the roses as much as she did.

"We don't have any roses in Kilshiel," Alasdair admitted, "but we've got other flowers. I'll show you some if you want."

"I'd like that." Milly's voice was a whisper on the wind. "Will I still have to be escorted in Kilshiel?"

"No, I don't think so. And I'm sorry about this. While we're in the wild, Kendrick doesn't want to let you out of his sight without knowing someone's with you."

"Is it to make sure I won't run away?"

"No! You're not a prisoner."

"I couldn't have refused to go with you." There was no bitterness in Milly's voice; it was simply a reminder of the truth.

"What do you mean?" Now Alasdair sounded confused. Conall, who was walking by his other side, twitched his ears. "If you didn't want to go, you could have..." He stopped talking and closed his eyes. "Barton said you *had* to. No wonder Kendrick's been acting so strangely."

Milly looked down at the grass. She could have refused. Right now, she could be back in Layden with her friends, preparing lunch or maybe eating it if the café was empty.

"Would you have said no?" Alasdair asked. "If Barton told you there was a choice, what would you have told him?"

Milly was silent for a long time. They kept walking through the trees, her hand delicately touching his arm. All she was aware of was the air as she breathed, the shapes of the trees they passed and the warmth of Alasdair's arm.

The truth was, she would have refused if she felt she could. But looking back over the evening with the Groves Wolf-Lords, the morning she saw the deer and the days spent walking through the land and seeing it...

Had she known about the experience that awaited her, she would have changed nothing. But she didn't want to admit it out loud.

"I'm not sure," she replied. "I know you said you don't have roses, but do you have any streams or rivers?"

Alasdair must have sensed she wanted to change the subject. "We've got a stream, but it's like ice. I fell it in once; I felt like I'd been frozen alive!"

"There's no chance of swimming?"

"Not in our water. Not even when it's warm enough."

Milly laughed. It was a light and carefree sound. As she peered through the gaps between the trees, she saw a hawk circling in the sky above them.

***

When Sami arrived in the library, Leo had a large piece of paper laid out on the table. Beside it lay two plain pencils and an eraser.

"Is that for your drawing classes?" she asked.

"Yeah." Leo picked up the pencils and studied them. "Not quite what paid artists get to work with, but these are pretty good. At least, I hope they are."

"You shouldn't complain, da Lange," Moira said. "You're lucky to even get drawing lessons here; do you know how many inmates in other correction facilities would like that?"

Leo looked down at the paper, lips pressed together. Moira gave a brief nod to Sami and walked out of the library.

In the left side of the room was a small bookcase marked MAPS. Sami drifted over and began to inspect them closely, pulling them off the shelves and checking which location they displayed. Maps of the countries themselves were on the top shelf, with Fearainn first and the islands of Tirmor on the far right. The next shelf down held maps of all the Fearainn towns and cities.

It didn't take long for Sami to locate three maps of Redcross. Two of them were yellow and very thin. She didn't want to risk opening them for fear of tearing the paper, so she very carefully slid them back onto the shelf.

One of the problems with walled cities was they never really changed. This meant although new houses could be built, the streets themselves weren't altered in any way. Sami wasn't sure how recently the third map had been drawn, but she hoped it could provide what they required.

She needed to approach this very carefully. "How are the classes, Leo?"

"Oh, they're fine. We're supposed to be working on complicated and intricate things now. She wants as much detail as possible."

Heart pounding, Sami unfolded the map, carried it over to the table and held it out to him. "Would this be intricate enough for her?"

Leo looked at the map, then at Sami's face.

Please, she mouthed silently.

"Yes," Leo said slowly. "I think that could be pretty challenging. She'd be very impressed if I drew that - even more if I drew two."

"Can you do that?"

Leo looked straight into Sami's eyes. "I'd better get started."

He pushed his piece of paper to one side of the table and carefully placed the map right next to it. Frowning, he looked at the centre of the map, then the paper, then back to the map again.

Sami watched as he picked up a pencil and began to sketch the main square, his eyes constantly darting from map to pencil to paper. Eventually, she chose a red book from the shelves, sat down and started to read. Every so often, her gaze would leave the page and focus on Leo as he concentrated.

***

"Avrel, it's your turn for the Complex today."

She groaned. "Thanks for reminding me." She was about to turn the stove on when something occurred to her. "Hey, Frankie, where did you say Debra is?"

"Thistleton House. I've got no idea where that is." Frankie brushed a stray wisp of hair out of her eyes, smudging her forehead with flour in the process.

"I do. It's close to the Complex; I think we walk by it every time we go there. Before I start my shift, I'll check on Debra and make sure she's OK."

"She'll be in an even worse state than you were when the wolves got here," Carlene said. "At least you've calmed down a bit."

"If you're going to check on her, you should go now," Sami pointed out. "Your shift starts in about half an hour."

Avrel quickly washed her hands, untied her apron and left it hanging on the right peg. "I'll see you all tomorrow!" she called as she left Layden's.

It was getting a bit warmer. The sun peeked out from behind gaps in the drifting clouds, but it wasn't strong enough to break through completely. Avrel kept walking until she found the right house: a building from red and grey bricks with two floors and windows at each one. Since it was one of the houses closest to the Complex, Avrel assumed Phoebe Macton might be one of the city's wealthier inhabitants, but someone who wasn't quite important enough for Barton to notice.

She went up to the maroon door and knocked twice, smiling politely as she waited for it to open.

Her smile dissolved in the heat of a furious glare. "Hi," she faltered. She cleared her throat, forcing herself to meet Phoebe's eyes. "I'm Avrel da Lange, a friend of Debra's. Is she in?"

"Oh, you're a friend of hers, are you? Good. Maybe you can talk her into finding something to do around here."

115

Phoebe pressed herself against the wall, allowing Avrel to step inside. Once she had, Phoebe closed the door and yelled: "Cameron! Some girl's here to see you."

Avrel walked towards the stairs. The air inside Thistleton House felt remarkably still and cold; the interior walls were painted dark blue, which gave her the impression of walking deeper and deeper into a tunnel.

She arrived at the base of the stairs and stood there, waiting, but nobody appeared at the top of them.

Behind her, Phoebe huffed in disgust.

Avrel looked at her nervously. "May I go up?" When the only response she got was a shrug, she climbed the stairs, her feet creaking on the wood beneath the carpet.

Facing her on the upper floor was a selection of closed doors. Just as Avrel was about to call Debra's name, one of them opened and Debra herself emerged. She let Avrel enter the bedroom, then shut the door.

The room was so empty. All it had was a single bed with a striped cover and a window. Avrel shivered and folded her arms, facing Debra.

"So you and your landlady don't get on," she said dryly.

Debra shook her head. She was pale, as if she hadn't slept for a very long time. Her collarbones stuck out and her fingers looked dangerously brittle. There were purple hollows under her dark eyes.

"Do they know?" she asked.

"No. If they did, they'd have confronted us *and* you."

Even as she spoke, Avrel felt uneasy. Wolves were predators; what if they were just biding their time, waiting for the right moment to attack?

"Is that blonde still with you?" Debra's voice was quiet and pleading.

"You mean Milly? No, she's got her own problems right now. We're trying to get you out of Redcross."

Debra's eyes suddenly went wild and fearful. She pushed past Avrel and opened the door, looking out at the empty hallway. After a moment, she shut the door again and faced Avrel.

"How?" she demanded.

"We're working on that. It might take a while."

Debra clenched her fists. "I can't stand this. I can't stand being cooped up. She's getting suspicious; she's

116

noticed I haven't left the house." She swallowed. "I thought I was safe here. When Barton announced the Andras Wolf-Lords were coming here, I didn't know who they were. I only knew Kendrick by his first name."

Avrel nodded, understanding completely. The fear she and the others felt was nothing compared to what Debra was going through.

"Do you know how long they're going to be here?" Debra asked.

"No. That's why we're thinking of a plan." Avrel smiled. She was trying to be reassuring, but Debra's tense posture didn't relax at all. "We'll get you out, Debra. That's a promise." She glanced out the window. "I'm sorry, but I have to go. One of us will be back soon. Just hold on."

She left the room and hurried down the stairs. Her shift was due to start in a few minutes and she hated being late for anything.

Just as she opened the front door, Phoebe said: "Wait one moment."

Avrel did so.

"You know how it goes in Redcross. You don't work, you don't eat."

Avrel nodded in reply.

"She does nothing in the house. She doesn't cook, she doesn't clean, she doesn't even try to find work. She doesn't do anything except sit in her room." Phoebe folded her arms, glaring down at Avrel. "She had better find something to do, or she won't be living here. Got it?"

"You'd better tell her that."

Avrel walked out of Thistleton House and firmly shut the door behind her.

***

"Sorry I'm late," Avrel panted as she entered the kitchen.

"Don't be silly, sweetheart. You're not late at all." Joyce handed Avrel an apron. "Do you remember how to make pea soup? The recipe is on the counter if you don't."

Avrel picked up the piece of paper. The last time she made this soup, she forgot she needed to add celery until it was almost too late.

"Don't use too much butter," Joyce said. "We're going

117

to need that."

"Sure." Avrel chopped three small onions and two stalks of celery into small pieces, then dropped a spoonful of butter into the pan and watched it melt. Nearby, Kaleb was preparing a chicken, with another one waiting close by.

Once the butter had surrendered to the heat, Avrel added the onion and the celery to soften them.

"Who's feeding the wolves now that Milly isn't?" she asked.

Kaleb shrugged without taking his eyes off the chicken. "The Wolf-Lords themselves, I guess."

"Is Milly all right?" Joyce asked, a worried frown creasing her brow. "Barton said she wouldn't be turning up for her shifts for a while."

Avrel said nothing. She just looked at Joyce, silently communicating everything she couldn't say out loud.

"Avrel, *is* she all right?" Joyce's voice was soft now.

We don't know, Avrel mouthed back. She turned around and stopped the onions from overcooking. Joyce slid the parsley across the counter to her, the frown still in place. Avrel nodded her thanks, telling herself it was the onions that were hurting her eyes.

Movement in the pantry made her jump. Tim, a worker from a café smaller than Layden's, left the tiny room, carrying a box of tomatoes that must have either come from the market or been delivered straight to the Complex.

"How many runners do you think they've caught?" he asked. "The Wolf-Lords, I mean."

"No idea," Joyce replied. "Could you wash those potatoes over there, Tim? If they're too small, ignore them."

"Seems a little weird the Premier would ask them over here just to deal with a couple of runners." Tim put the box of tomatoes on the chopping table in the middle of the kitchen and walked over to the sink. He turned on the taps just as Kaleb let out a small, derisive chuckle.

Immediately, Tim turned the taps off. "What? What's so funny?"

"Twenty Wolf-Lords don't come all the way from their village to deal with *runners*. There's got to be a bigger reason."

"Why are they here?" Tim asked.

"None of our business," Joyce said briskly. "Avrel, watch your onions."

"Sorry."

The smells of cooking filled the kitchen, but Avrel could barely concentrate. She spent the entirety of her shift in a confused daze. If the Wolf-Lords weren't in Redcross to help Barton deal with runners and they didn't come to the city to deliberately hunt down a runaway girl, why were they here?

Chapter 13

When she lived in Kindainn, Milly had watched the land wake up as winter slowly withdrew. There wasn't time for that in Redcross, so she settled for watching the city wake up each morning after an enforced sleep.

Now Fearainn was alive, and she loved being in it.

"I don't understand why they even built the walled cities," Sorcha said one afternoon. She dipped a large T-shirt into the river several times and wrung it out; droplets of water ran down her bare arms. "I mean, I know why – I just don't understand why nobody's knocked the walls down for good."

"Because they were afraid," was Milly's reply, "or maybe because the walls were part of the city by then." Her fingers were wet and slightly numb. The clothes she and Sorcha had already washed were draped over tree branches, drying in sunlight that somehow escaped through the leaves. Milly's pink and blue clothes stood out sharply among the darker clothes worn by the Wolf-Lords.

"They're just our travelling clothes," Sorcha told her. "When we get back to Kilshiel, it'll be so good to wear actual colours again."

Lyall lay sprawled beside Sorcha. The girl grinned and flicked some water into the wolf's face; startled, Lyall growled and shook her head, spraying drops everywhere. Sorcha laughed and stroked the furry black head.

"If anyone who wasn't me tried that, she'd have their hand off!"

Milly looked at Lyall's jaws, and knew it wasn't a lie.

"You were saying you've got sisters."

Milly nodded. "They're both older than me. Rachel's working as an artist and Susanna's at the Academy." She wondered if Susanna had written again, and what their parents would say in the reply.

"An artist *and* an Academic? In one family? In Kilshiel, it's an honour to have two Wolf-Lords in two generations in one family. It's rare, too."

"Is it in the blood?"

"No. It doesn't matter if your mother or father, aunt or

uncle, brother or sister is a Wolf-Lord. Anyone in Kilshiel can become one, if a wolf cub picks them." Sorcha spotted something at the base of a nearby tree close to the river. "Look at this."

Milly followed her over, the grass cold under her bare feet.

Sorcha pointed at a tiny mushroom. "See that ridge on the stem? That's one way to tell if a mushroom's deadly or not. If it's got one of those anywhere, it's poisonous. Same if it's got red on the cap or the stem."

"Are those the only ways to tell if you can eat a mushroom or not?"

"No. If we see another one, I'll tell you if it's safe to eat. If I'm not sure it's safe, we'll leave it alone." Sorcha got to her feet and stepped backward - and tripped over a tree root. She shrieked and fell into the river.

"Sorcha!" Milly saw a pale hand reaching up and clutching at nothing before being swept away. There was no time to be afraid, no time to think. She jumped in.

The cold stole her breath. It stung her eyes. She kicked her legs, trying to catch up with Sorcha. She could barely see her through the dark, rushing water and her lungs were starting to burn. This river was much fiercer and faster than the ones in Kindainn.

Milly's head broke the surface; she took a desperate gulp of air before plunging back under and swimming as fast as she could. If the river became much deeper, she might never find Sorcha.

There she was. Her legs were caught in a clump of weeds; Sorcha was splashing her arms around to keep her head above the surface. Milly acted quickly. She grabbed a tree root sticking out in her way and used it to pull herself close to the side, inching her way towards the terrified Sorcha.

If they both became trapped in the weeds, neither would make it.

Her fingers closed around something. It was a stone with a pointed end. The clump was only a small one. Milly breathed in, locked her knees and one hand around the nearest root and dove back under. Clutching the stone tightly, she swiped at the weeds around Sorcha's legs; little by little, strand by strand, they gave way until her left leg was free.

At that moment, the weed around Sorcha's right leg snapped. Milly grabbed at the other girl's ankle and held on with all her strength. Her shoulder screamed with the weight and spots danced in her vision, but she managed to pull Sorcha over to the side.

"What do we do now?" Sorcha could barely speak through chattering teeth.

"We get out," Milly coughed. With every ounce of her remaining strength, she used the root and handfuls of grass to heave herself out of the river.

Black paws skidded to a stop. Lyall grabbed the back of Sorcha's T-shirt and pulled her onto the bank beside Milly. The girls lay side by side, panting heavily.

Milly sat up, her wet clothes sticking uncomfortably to her body. "Where are we?"

"I don't know." Sorcha's voice was a barely audible rasp. She huddled up to Lyall and wrapped her arms around her, shivering violently.

Milly drew her knees under her and gripped her feet with her hands, trying to drive some warmth into them. "We need to get moving. If we start walking, we can get warmer faster."

"But where *are* we?" asked Sorcha.

They were surrounded by a maze of trees. Milly didn't recognise any of them.

Fear colder than the river punctured her heart.

"If we go in the opposite direction the river's flowing, we'll find the clothes. Find the clothes, we find the others." She started walking, taking care to keep away from the water's edge. Sorcha and Lyall followed her.

Milly was both glad and furious that they'd taken their shoes off. Shoes would have weighed them down in the water, but the grass was still slippery and hidden twigs and pebbles were painful on bare soles.

A loud howl made Milly's heart jolt. Lyall howled again, her cry echoing around them until it seemed to fill the forest.

"We shouldn't be that far away," Milly said, looking back at Sorcha. All the same, she heard the doubt in her own voice; the girls could have been swept much farther than she thought they had.

Suddenly there were howls reaching through the air. Lyall bounded away from Sorcha and ahead of Milly; she jumped over a mossy rock and howled again.

"They're coming," Sorcha breathed. "They'll find us."

"Should we stay and wait, or keep going?"

Lyall looked expectantly over her shoulder, her eyes bright.

"Keep going!"

The girls started jogging, steadily growing warmer even as the wind whipped through their hair and tangled it. If her feet were cut by stones or twigs, Milly didn't feel it. Air filled her lungs until she thought they would burst.

Then wolves burst through the trees and surrounded them, Aela at their head. Lyall let out tiny, relieved whines as she licked Aela's muzzle.

Andras wasn't far behind them. "Are you both all right? What happened?"

"We fell in the river," Milly said.

"No, I fell in." Sorcha jabbed a finger at Milly. "*She* jumped in after me. Thank you so much for saving me, Emilia."

Milly avoided looking at Andras' face. "Why didn't Lyall try to jump in?"

"She can't swim. Hates water." Sorcha started laughing. "Of all the wolves, I get the one who hates water!"

"It's not funny, Sorcha!" Andras snapped. "We need to get you some dry clothes and then build a fire."

"But we washed most of our clothes," protested Sorcha.

"Then you can borrow some!" Andras replied, looking pointedly at her. "Someone might have shoes in your..." He looked down at Milly's bare feet, then at Sorcha's. He shrugged off his jacket and handed it to Milly, saying: "Edan, could you give Sorcha your fleece?"

Once she had the jacket on, Milly wrapped her arms around herself, grateful for the warmth.

"I'm sorry about this, Emilia."

Andras stepped forward and picked Milly up by the waist, tossing her onto his shoulder.

"Hey, what..." Milly's protest died as the wind blew across her feet. Sacrificing her dignity instead of walking back without shoes felt like a better idea, even if it hadn't been hers.

"All right if I carry your lady, Lyall?" Edan asked.

"Do you have to?" whined Sorcha.

"Do you want to walk like that?" Andras asked pointedly. One arm was around the back of Milly's legs, keeping her in place.

"...No."

There was a brief pause, then Andras said: "Let's go."

***

The two girls spent a while in front of a fire, huddled in blankets. Once Milly looked up to see Brochan and Andras arguing quietly. She couldn't hear what they were saying, yet something about their expressions gave her a sense of unease.

She coughed, covering her mouth to hide the sound.

"Hey." Alasdair knelt beside her. "Are you all right?"

"I'm fine. Thanks. Could I have some more water, please?" Her bottle stood empty next to her. She could still feel the river's chill and her throat was as dry as a stone. No matter how much water Milly drank, she still wasn't satisfied. She wrapped the blanket tighter around herself, wanting to get closer to the fire.

Alasdair frowned. "That's the second time you've needed more water." He reached out with one hand. Milly flinched back; Alasdair paused, his hand in the air between them.

"I just want to feel your forehead and neck," he said. "I'm not going to hurt you."

Slowly, Milly relaxed. Alasdair pressed the back of his hand to first her forehead, then her throat. "You're warm."

"I'm next to a fire."

Alasdair shuffled over to Sorcha and, after asking permission, felt her forehead and throat as well. "Sorcha's next to the fire as well and she's not half as warm as you."

"And I haven't gone red, either," Sorcha said.

"Wait there." Alasdair got up and went over to Alasdair and Brochan. Milly was unable to hear his voice, but she saw his lips move to form the words *I think we've got a problem.* All three turned to look at Milly.

There was fear on Andras and Alasdair's faces.

***

The next town was two days away. They moved as fast as they could, and they still didn't get there in time.

***

There was a faint amber blur. It became brighter or dimmed when Milly moved her head. It stayed bright if she kept her face turned to the right, with her cheek resting against something soft.

Someone was bathing her forehead earlier. She remembered that.

After minutes that felt like hours, or hours that felt like minutes, her eyelids slowly opened by themselves.

The amber blur came from a lamp close beside her; the glow spread across the room like a sunset. A small glass of water had been placed beside the lamp. Milly tried to sit up but her head felt far too light; she lay back down and took deep breaths until the dizziness faded. Someone had dressed her in a thick nightgown with sleeves that ran down to her wrists. Her neck was faintly clammy with sweat.

"Where..." She coughed, reached for the glass and took a sip. The water went all the way down to her stomach, making her shiver. She put the glass back on the table and wriggled her arm back under the cover.

"Hello?" she called. Her voice sounded weak and thin.

The door opened, spilling a brighter light into the room. A woman in a brown dress entered; immediately, her face broke into a beaming smile. "Oh, good! You're awake!" She looked back over her shoulder and called: "Celia! Tell them she's awake!"

Milly faintly heard someone hurrying away, their footsteps growing fainter in the distance.

"You're probably wondering where you are, aren't you?" the woman said. She walked up to the bedside and smiled down at Milly. "You're in Dalnair. My name's Heather - how are you feeling?"

"I'm fine."

"How are you really feeling?" Heather pressed.

125

"Like all the strength's gone out of me."

"That's to be expected. You've had a fever for three days; you're lucky they brought you here."

Milly reached up to brush a hand through her hair. Her fingers met a damp mass of tangles and she lowered it, tucking her arm back beneath the cover. There were no windows in the room, which meant she couldn't tell if it was daylight, dusk or night outside. Her eyelids were heavy. They began to drift downwards.

A loud yelp of "Hey!" came from the other side of the door; a moment later, Heather shrank back as Conall burst into the bedroom, Alasdair close behind him.

"Emilia!" Alasdair breathed. The lamplight made his eyes shine as bright as the sun.

Andras stepped inside. He was smiling. "You gave us a bit of a scare, Emilia."

"I'm sorry," Milly croaked. "I'm sorry for slowing you down."

Andras shook his head firmly. "You saved Sorcha's life. It could have been her in bed with a fever - or it could have been both of you. All you have to do now is rest until you're up for travelling again; it doesn't matter how long that takes."

He stepped closer to the bed and sat on a chair beside it. "On behalf of all of us, thank you." "Thank you for helping *me*."

"I meant what I said. Get as much rest as you need." He put a hand on Milly's shoulder, smiled once more and made for the door.

Milly couldn't let them go just yet. "Wait."

Both Andras and Alasdair stopped. Conall's ears twitched.

"Please call me Milly," she said softly.

"We will if you call him Kendrick." Alasdair jerked his thumb towards the taller Wolf-Lord.

Milly smiled. "I think I can do that."

Chapter 14

"Joyce was right. It's none of our business," Sami said firmly. "As long as they're not investigating us or Debra, we don't need to worry about them."

"But you have to admit, it's really intriguing." Carlene carefully flipped the sausages over onto their uncooked sides. "What's the biggest security threat to Redcross, if it's not the runners? And why would Barton lie about it?"

"Actually, he didn't lie," Frankie realised. "I don't think he ever said what the Wolf-Lords would be doing. We just assumed he meant the runners and *only* the runners."

"Sami's got a point," Avrel said, "but we do need to worry. My dad says to never trust a leader who is deliberately keeping secrets."

"What if the secrets are for our good?" Sami asked worriedly.

"Barton doesn't seem like the kind of person who'd keep a secret for somebody's protection. I know it's just a rumour but if Kaleb's figured out something might be wrong, who else has?" Carlene asked. She checked Layden's door just in case someone was about to come in, or the couple sitting at the far end was in danger of overhearing them. "Why don't you talk to your friend Nicholas, Frankie? He's the new head of security; he's bound to know..."

"He is not my friend," Frankie retorted, "and there's no way I'm going to deliberately talk to him about anything."

"Why are you so scared of him?" asked Carlene. "I think you're more frightened of him than you are of the Wolf-Lords. What did he do?"

"You never said what the incident was," Sami added. "All you've ever said is he hates you because of it."

Frankie glared at them both defensively. "Does it matter what the incident was? If I talk to him, he'll realise something's wrong *because* I'm talking to him."

"What about Jason's brother?" Sami suggested. "He's a Watchman. He might know what's happening."

"Oh, now you want to know what's going on?" Avrel said sceptically.

Sami flushed. "Like Carlene said, it's a rumour, but..." She dropped the used cutlery she was holding in the sink and sighed heavily. "Maybe we should find out if it *is* something we need to worry about. It might affect the whole city. If we don't learn the truth, someone like Kaleb will."

The door to the café opened; Carlene hurried out to greet the customer and all conversation in the kitchen ceased.

The silence didn't last long.

"How's Leo?" Frankie asked casually, going to rescue the sausages Carlene had left unattended.

"He's fine. He's working on both maps now. And," Avrel said, her voice trembling slightly, "Mum and Dad said they might go and visit him."

"That's fantastic! It's...wait, maps? What maps?"

"We're going to use one to get Debra out of here; the other is for Leo's art classes," Sami said.

Frankie placed the sausages between two buttered slices of warm bread, put the plates onto a tray and hurried out to serve the waiting couple. When she returned, she said: "There's just one problem. How are you going to get the map out of the facility?"

"Simple," Avrel shrugged. "We'll just tell the guards Leo drew it for us."

Frankie blinked several times, mouth hanging open. "Oh. Yes. That would work. And what's more, it'd be true! But it's so great your parents are going to see Leo."

"I said they *might*. They haven't said they *will*." But there was a glimmer of hope in Avrel's eyes that hadn't been there before.

"How long has he got left on his sentence?"

"Six months. But that means we've got to be careful. It's not just ourselves, Carlene and Debra we're putting at risk. It's Leo. If we get caught with that map..." Avrel's voice trailed off and she looked down at the floor. Frankie and Sami glanced at each other, each girl's face mirroring the other's anxiety.

***

"Take the afternoon off."

"Are you serious?" Frankie asked.

"You can't rely completely on Leo's map. What if he doesn't get it finished in time? The reason Jason hasn't been caught is he knows the city so well. And if you're planning to run at night, you might not even be able to *see* the map."

Frankie grimaced. "Good point. Are you sure things will be OK if I do go?"

"Absolutely."

It would probably take Frankie the rest of the day to walk around half the city; if she timed it right, she would be on her way home before the drums. The only question was where to begin.

She began to walk towards the main gates. Once she reached them, she swerved sharply to the right and kept going along the walls. She had only gone a few paces when she looked back over her shoulder, just to check the guards weren't watching her.

They were looking straight ahead of them, as still as statues.

The city grew quieter as Frankie walked. Before long, the only sounds were her soft footsteps and the birds outside.

She could hear *birds*.

If she closed her eyes and listened, she could almost imagine herself back on the island with her friend Jack and the other children. But she didn't close her eyes. She couldn't, because she had a job to do.

Eventually, after walking past houses with paint peeling from the walls and windows that wept broken glass, she came across a small gate. It was simple and wooden, with a single metal latch. There was no way to tell if it was locked from the outside, or if anyone was standing guard on the other side. Frankie needed to find out, but if there *was* someone on the other side of the gate, they would want to know why she was there.

It was a risk she couldn't take, so she walked away.

As she did so, she found her mind wandering back to her life on the island. Frankie's mother, Arabella, was born in Redcross and moved to the Gull Islands after marrying Frankie's father.

Frankie didn't have a lot of memories of her father; he

drowned when she was three years old, leaving Arabella to raise their young daughter alone on an island that was starting to feel like a cage.

When Barton's letter came, Arabella didn't hesitate to respond.

Unlike her mother, Frankie had loved living on the island. Given the choice, she would rather live her life surrounded by sea than by walls, but she loved her friends in Redcross as well and things wouldn't be the same if she went back to live on the island.

Her home had been on the largest of the Gull Islands. It was covered in small hills, with rocks surrounded by long, dry grass dancing in the sea air. In evening, when the sun was going down, it provided the perfect hiding places.

"There he is." Jack's voice was barely louder than the rustling grass, which was almost black in the setting sun. The sun itself was retreating behind pink and violet clouds, casting a golden sheen on the water behind the children. "Go on, Pips."

"No! I can't do it!"

"What's the matter?" Jack jeered. "Are you scared?"

"No," mumbled Pips. "I just don't want him to catch me."

If Frankie peered over the small hill, she knew she would see a solitary figure walking around, completely at ease, long hair as free as the wind. He didn't know they were there - yet - and it wasn't time for them to go home, so nobody was worried about their whereabouts.

"I'll go." Keeping low to the ground, Frankie crept around the hill. As soon as she was out in the open, her heart started beating faster than a rabbit's. Slowly, she moved on her hands and knees, deliberately not disturbing the grass too much.

Nicholas looked her way. She flattened herself to the ground, grass scratching her cheek and palms. If he saw her, the game would be over.

Frankie knew the island as well as she knew herself. The only problem was that Nicholas did as well and Frankie was seriously beginning to dislike the way he always seemed to be watching her. Before that stupid incident, it was only Jack he'd keep an eye on.

If she stayed quiet and didn't make too many rustling

sounds, he wouldn't have any idea where she was.

She inched forward little by little, not daring to raise her eyes and knowing she would have to. She just hoped when she did, she wouldn't see his eyes looking back at her.

Frankie snapped out of her memories. Somehow, she had meandered onto one of the four main roads. Maybe if she walked back into the main part of town again, she would find another exit.

She walked down the broad pathway, past a Wolf-Lord and through a large, empty street with shops on either side. From the looks of things, most of them hadn't been open in...

Frankie stopped dead, shock flooding her veins. That was a Wolf-Lord. She walked right past a Wolf-Lord and didn't even blink. She'd grown used to them, just as she'd grown used to the Watchmen. How had *that* happened?

Nicholas Ainsley was different. Carlene was right: Frankie was more afraid of him than she was of the Wolf-Lords.

Frankie stopped walking and gazed ahead of her, a confused frown on her face. Now she was thinking about it, she wasn't sure she knew *why* she feared him so much.

She wasn't a little girl now. He wasn't the nemesis she remembered from the island, and it didn't matter anyway. He would be gone as soon as Trevel returned.

As soon as Debra was away from the city, all Frankie and the others needed to do was wait until the Wolf-Lords and Nicholas left. Then everything would go back to how it should be.

Frankie started walking again, knowing deep down her hopes wouldn't come to pass. Nothing was ever going to be normal again.

***

"There it is," Alasdair said. "That's Kilshiel." His voice was as warm as the sun above.

Kilshiel was a little smaller than Malnaig, with thatched houses made from grey stone. Each house was near enough to the next one to create a sense of closeness, but just far enough away to give the inhabitants some privacy. Right in the centre of the village was a hall built out of the same grey stone. Grass grew all around the houses; clumps of heather stuck out on the green carpet like jewels.

"They're back!" "They're home!"

Joy and delight echoed in the air as the people of Kilshiel hurried out to welcome their loved ones back home.

Milly stopped, suddenly reluctant to take another step.

"Hey," Alasdair murmured. "It's OK."

Milly gave him a small, shaky smile. She wanted to stay as close to Alasdair as she possibly could. Out of all the Wolf-Lords, he was the most familiar and she felt safe with him.

"Thank you," she whispered.

The Wolf-Lords rushed to embrace their families and friends. Edan caught up a little boy with the same dark hair as him and swung the child around before placing a kiss on his wife's lips. Sorcha was being hugged by two people at the same time, while Lyall looked on with an expression of extreme patience.

"Stay beside me," Kendrick told Milly. "I need to introduce you properly."

Eventually the noise of the reunions faded into silence. Milly stood up straight, hands at her sides, looking as many people as she could in the eye.

"Everyone, I'd like you to meet Milly Costello," Kendrick said. Milly smiled and nodded.

"You brought someone back?" A young woman about Susanna's age stepped forward. Her braided hair was like sun on autumn leaves.

"Just like I said I would," Kendrick replied.

"She looks so...delicate." The young woman said the word *delicate* as if it repulsed her.

"Aela approved," Kendrick said firmly. "And this isn't the first long journey Milly's been on. I'd say she handled it admirably. Could you show her where she'll be staying, Tamira?"

The redhead nodded, glanced once at Milly and walked towards one of the small houses.

"How long are you going to be here?" she asked when Milly caught up with her. It was surprisingly difficult to keep pace with Tamira, but Milly managed to walk beside her nonetheless.

"Six months." Milly wasn't sure if the six months started today now that she had officially arrived at Kilshiel, or if they had begun the moment she stepped outside Redcross.

Tamira nodded thoughtfully. "Six months. That's a reasonable time." She opened the door of the house and held it for Milly. "Come and see your new home."

The inside of the house was painted white, with soft-looking red chairs and a blackened fireplace. The bedroom door was open; Milly saw a bed with a dark green cover and a window opening out to the sky.

"There's no kitchen," she said.

"You won't be needing one. I'll have someone bring you in some logs. Do you know how to light a fire?"

"I've seen someone else do it."

"Don't burn the house down. Sorry I can't help you settle properly, but we've got a guest coming tonight. I need to get her room sorted."

Just as Milly walked further into the house, Tamira took her arm. She wasn't rough, but it was enough to make Milly stop and look right into the other girl's piercing eyes.

"There's something about you," Tamira said, "and I'm not sure what. I'm going to say this now: I didn't like the one Gabrielle brought back. Whatever secrets you're keeping might be just your concern and if they are, that's fine. But if you hurt any of us in any way, it won't only be me you'll have to deal with. Kendrick can't afford for you to mess up. You'd better be the right choice for this."

There was a note of warning in her tone.

Tamira held Milly's gaze for one more moment, then she released her arm and left the house, closing the door behind her.

133

Chapter 15

Sami held the small box carefully, ignoring the wind biting her fingers. The clouds overhead hinted it would rain and she wanted to get inside the facility before the downpour started. If the box got wet, so would the item inside it.

The Watchmen at the gate were sheltered from any rain by a small canopy above their heads. One of them nodded at Sami as she approached. "Here to see da Lange?"

"Yes."

"Go right on...what's in the box?" he demanded. "It's just a little something from Layden's." Sami opened the box and showed the Watchman what was inside. Frankie had set it aside specially for Leo.

"Well, I hope he's grateful for that. Are you expected?" Sami was used to these questions by now.

"I am."

Moira was waiting for her inside the facility. "Right on time, Samara. Da Lange is in the library, as usual." She looked at the box and raised a single eyebrow at Sami. "Mind if I take a look?"

"Not at all," Sami replied, opening the box again. She sincerely hoped Leo would like the treat. Frankie had spent ages deciding which tart was the best one, much to Carlene's irritation.

Moira inspected the contents of the box briefly, then nodded and walked in the direction of the library, Sami just behind her.

"The doors are going to be closed this time."

"Seriously?"

"We've decided we can trust you. If we get any inkling that we can't, the doors are open again. Do you understand?"

"Completely." Sami's voice was serene, but she couldn't stop a thrill of excitement coursing through her. They might be able to talk more freely behind a closed door.

That didn't mean they could take any further risks.

"I think it's colder outside than it is in here," she remarked.

Moira glanced back at her and smiled. "Maybe you're right."

Leo sat at the library table, the map of Redcross spread over one half and one of his drawings on the other. His brow was furrowed in a frown of concentration as his eyes darted between the two.

"She's here, da Lange," Moira announced. "Remember, no funny business."

The door closed behind Sami. She stood where she was with the box cradled in her hands, unsure why the library was suddenly so still and quiet, and why she felt deeply, deeply vulnerable.

"Hi," she said. "Look what I got you."

She walked over to him and held out the small box. Leo opened it and his smile widened when he saw the perfect strawberry tart inside.

"I know it's not pink sugar ice cream," Sami continued, "but it's the best I could do." She sat on the chair opposite his, right on the other side of the table.

"Wow." Leo looked down at the map anxiously. "I guess I'd better eat this quickly before I get stains on the paper."

"Then you're lucky I brought this." Sami pulled a clean napkin out of her pocket and passed it over to him.

As soon as Leo bit into the tart, a smile spread over his face and he made a noise of deep enjoyment. Crumbs fell onto his lap, but he paid them no attention. "How come she makes these so perfectly?"

"Because she loves doing it." Sami watched as Leo continued to eat. It was as if he was tasting the effort and enjoyment Frankie put into making the tarts and savouring every memory she recalled in the process. The tarts were saturated with her love for the island and the people living on it.

Leo stopped chewing, raised his eyes to meet Sami's, and in that moment all she could see was his gaze. It stole the breath from her.

"I'm sorry," Leo said. "I didn't offer you any."

"I don't mind. I've already had one and..."

Leo made a motion with his hand, holding the remnants of the tart out to her in his open palm. Then he set it carefully on the arm of his chair and leaned towards

135

Sami. She stood up, leaned forwards as well and suddenly his lips were against hers.

It only lasted a moment. She moved backwards and found herself looking into his dark eyes again.

"I would say sorry for that," Leo murmured, "but I won't."

"I'm not sorry we did that either," Sami said quietly, in case the sound carried through the closed door, "but I think Moira might call that *funny business* and I'd like to keep coming back here."

She wasn't sorry...but she did feel guilty for betraying Moira's trust.

Gently, she took Leo's hand. Leo nodded, squeezed her hand and released it. She sat back down and took the nearest book from the shelves without even looking at the title. Leo picked up a pencil and started studying the map closely, using his free hand to scoop up the last of the tart.

When Moira opened the door to check on them, she found them in complete silence, absorbed in what they were doing. Neither of them looked up when she closed the door again.

***

Milly stretched lazily and opened her eyes. It felt so good to sleep in a bed again. The green bedcover was soft and warm, but not thick or heavy. She swung her legs over the side of the bed, wincing as her feet touched cold stone.

Milly got dressed in her warmer jeans, a blue T-shirt and her fleece before slowly opening the front door of the house.

The sunrise was almost finished melting into a grey sky. As Milly stepped outside, she saw people walking around carrying buckets. They must have been to the stream Alasdair mentioned. Milly thought she remembered seeing a bucket next to the fireplace; it wouldn't do any harm to find out where the stream was located, and she could always come back to it later. She didn't want her first walk in the area to be one that involved a bucket.

"Excuse me," she called softly to the nearest person. He stopped walking; water sloshed over the rim of the bucket he was carrying. "Where do I find the stream?"

He jerked his head in the direction of three large, rugged hills. "Over that way. Just keep walking and you'll come across it, lass."

"Thank you."

The inhabitants of Kilshiel had gone to the stream so many times they had worn a small path in the grass. Milly stepped on it carefully, keeping her eyes on where the furrow was leading her. The three hills slowly grew larger as she neared them.

The furrow faded but Milly kept walking, leaving the houses behind her. She heard the stream before she saw it; the clear ribbon of water seemed to dance, tinkling softly like crystal.

A soft rumble of thunder made Milly look up to the sky just as rain began to fall. She closed her eyes and breathed in the air before throwing her arms wide and spinning around on the spot, laughing as the rain danced around her.

After a few wild, glorious moments, she stopped and opened her eyes.

Alasdair stood a short way away, staring at Milly. He awkwardly held up a bucket in one hand. "I was just..." He lowered his hand slowly. "You'll be missed back there."

"Why?" Milly asked. "We're not on the journey now. I don't have to be anywhere."

Alasdair was looking at her as if she were crazy.

Milly realised he probably thought she was. But she didn't care about that. Her arms were slowly growing cold and yet she couldn't stop herself from smiling. "I'll see you later."

She turned around and walked away. The wind blew stronger, streaming her hair behind her. Rain spattered down on her, but she didn't care about that either. She wanted to stay outside for as long as she could. If she stretched her arms out again, she knew she would almost feel the wind carrying her.

"Where are you going?" Alasdair demanded. "Breakfast starts soon!"

Milly spun around to face him again. "I lived behind walls for two years. Do you know how badly I've wanted to feel the rain like this? To be *outside*?"

"What's going on?" Kendrick stood behind Alasdair, holding a bucket in one hand.

"Nothing," Alasdair said after a moment. He looked at Milly apologetically. "Nothing's going on. Milly just wanted some air."

It was only now Milly noticed Conall and Aela weren't there. She wanted to ask where they were, but there was clearly nothing to worry about. The wolves couldn't be beside their humans all the time.

"Come on," Kendrick said. "They're just cooking breakfast."

"Will there be porridge?" Milly asked. She watched as Alasdair and Kendrick used the buckets to scoop some water from the stream.

"There always is."

They started back towards Kilshiel. A few moments of companionable silence passed before Alasdair asked: "Is Aela looking forward to having her picture painted?"

"I think so. She can sit still for hours - unless the picture is of her standing, in which case there might be a problem."

"What's the background going to be? Mountains, or a moonlit night?" Milly didn't think the artist would draw Aela with blood dripping from her jaws; the last wolves to be painted like that had fought in the wars and as far as she was aware, Kendrick hadn't fought against or killed anyone.

"Probably a moonlit night."

"That will look so beautiful with her fur! Tamira said there was a guest at Kilshiel. Is that the artist?"

Kendrick nodded. "We couldn't get a well-known artist, but this one's said to be very talented."

Just then, the rain decided it was bored with falling lightly and wanted to be less kind to the walkers.

"Run!" Kendrick shouted. They raced the rest of the way back to Kilshiel, their hair and clothes slowly becoming wetter and wetter. Water sloshed over the side of Kendrick and Alasdair's buckets. By the time they reached the village, all three of them were thoroughly soaked and laughing joyfully. The man Milly had asked about the spring stifled a smile at the sight of them; Brochan shook his head and turned away.

A figure was waiting for them in the hall. "Hi!" she said brightly. "Great to meet you, Kendrick! I can't wait to...Milly?"

Milly couldn't believe it. She stared ahead of her in shock.

"Rachel?"

Chapter 16

Rachel rushed forwards and crushed Milly in a tight hug. "What are you *doing* here?" she cried.

"How do you know each other?" Alasdair asked, looking between the two of them.

"Milly's my sister!" Rachel's face was brighter than the light in the hall. "I know we don't look like we're related, but believe me, we are."

"Wait...*you're* the artist! Milly's told me about you!" said Sorcha as she hurried up to them. "And the middle girl's Susanna, isn't she?"

"She is! I hope Milly's been telling you good things about us." Rachel kept an arm around her sister's shoulders. "But seriously, what *are* you doing here? You're supposed to be back in Redcross - are Mum and Dad here too?"

"No," Milly said slowly. "I'm on my own. I'm a...I'm a guest here."

Rachel looked down at her. "How long for?" she asked, raising her eyes to meet Kendrick's.

"Six months," was his reply.

"I see. Well, I'm only staying for as long as it takes to paint...what's his name?"

"Aela."

Rachel nodded. "Aela. Sorry. I promise I'll do the best job I can."

"I can't wait to see the picture when it's finished." Milly had never seen her sister's professional paintings before, only sketches and coloured pencil drawings.

"I can't wait to show it to you. Would you mind if I borrowed my sister during breakfast?" Rachel asked Kendrick. "There's a lot we need to catch up on."

"She's welcome to sit with whoever she likes."

Minutes later, the sisters were sitting together at a small table, bowls of porridge in front of them.

"Not quite like Mum's, is it?" Rachel asked, cutting a red and green apple into tiny, perfect chunks.

"Nope." Milly ate a spoonful and thought it was almost as good as their mother's. "But then, it's just porridge. I guess anything tastes good if you love the person who made it."

"Remember when Susy tried baking bread that time and she left it in the oven too long? It looked like a husk. How is she, by the way?" Rachel put the knife down on the table. "I know she writes to you. It's hard to get a message when you're not staying long in one place."

"The last one was short. She said to give you her love, and I think she might have met someone."

"Really?" Rachel grinned impishly.

"She hasn't said she has, but she keeps mentioning someone called Edwin. Oh, and the food isn't as good as Mum's," Milly said.

"This man paid me a lot to paint his son, only the kid wouldn't stay still! His mum had to keep telling him to stay on the stool and if he did, he'd get some chocolate." Rachel peered around the hall, eyes narrowed. "Speaking of painting subjects, when do I get to meet Aela?"

"Soon, I think," Milly said. "She's not as fierce as she seems, I promise."

Rachel looked at her sister as if she'd never seen her before. "Milly, she's a *wolf*."

***

"What background would you like?" Milly thought she saw Rachel's hands tremble slightly as she arranged her brushes on the little square table she'd been given for her task. In front of the chair was a wooden stand; Milly couldn't see what her sister was going to be painting on.

"Could you paint a forest at night?"

"With a moon shining through the trees?"

Kendrick nodded.

Rachel looked around the stand at Aela, who was in the ideal position: standing with her body horizontal to the artist's perspective, with her head turned towards her.

Rachel would have the perfect view of Aela's eyes. "That'll work. I'm going to paint her first, then do the background."

Kendrick ran a hand down Aela's back, looking into her eyes. The air was filled with words neither man nor wolf spoke aloud.

Milly quietly stepped out of the small house. She wanted to watch her sister paint, yet it seemed a private moment between artist, Wolf-Lord and wolf and she had no right to be there. She turned around and nearly collided with Tamira, who was walking right past her.

"Sorry!" Milly moved to go around her.

"It's all right." Tamira's hair was wet from the rain. "Are they in there?" She pointed towards the house doorway.

"Yes. They'd be painting outside if it wasn't raining. What did..." Milly stopped, embarrassed. She couldn't refer to Weatherhill by her last name in front of someone who had known her well.

Tamira waited for her to continue.

"What background did Kendrick's predecessor use?"

"She used mountains. A lot of *teaghlach* leaders have mountains in their wolves' pictures."

"What was she like?" When Milly was fifteen, Weatherhill had been fearsome. Now two years had passed and she didn't seem so frightening in Milly's memory.

Tamira glanced at a nearby doorway. She beckoned to Milly and hurried over to the shelter. Once they were safely under the stone archway, she said: "Gabrielle was very secretive. Not a lot of people knew what she was really like; I think that's the way she wanted it." She frowned. "There may have been one person."

Milly said nothing. She merely waited.

Tamira gazed out over the village. "I'm only telling you this because she's not here anymore. If she was, I'd be keeping my mouth shut and I'm trusting you're going to do the same even after you leave."

"I will."

"One time, she was part of a visit to the Groves Wolf-Lords. I can't remember what it was about, but when they all came back Gabrielle wasn't the same. She was even more withdrawn than before. I overheard Brochan telling someone Gabrielle became...attached to one of the Groves lot."

"It must have been more than an attachment," Milly said.

"It was, on her part. Brochan never said what the man's name was. All he said was the other Wolf-Lord

142

might have been planning to come back here with Gabrielle. When Matthias Groves found out, he and the Wolf-Lord had a private talk and Gabrielle returned without him."

"Matthias made him stay?"

Tamira shrugged. "I don't know. He might have done - or he could have advised him to think carefully before making a decision that was based on knowing someone for only a few days. That's what I would have done. Anyway, I hear the artist is your sister?"

"I still can't believe she's here! We haven't seen her for a long time." Milly looked up at the taller young woman. "Do you have brothers or sisters?"

"No, just one cousin. He went down to Redcross with the others, except he's staying there until this little problem's been taken care of." With an expression of deep reluctance on her face, Tamira said: "I need to go and help get lunch ready."

"I could help, if you want. I worked in a café and I learn recipes pretty quickly."

"Do you?" Tamira's lips moved into what looked like half a smile. "All right. Come with me and we'll see what you can really do."

She led Milly into the hall, across the empty eating area and into the kitchen. Immediately, Milly heard bubbling water and smelled meat cooking. She wasn't surprised to see there were no wolves in the room.

"Our little guest has offered to help," Tamira announced. "Do you think we can find her something to do?"

The challenge echoed in the room.

***

"It's so hot in here," Avrel moaned, swiping her forehead. Strands of hair were stuck to her skin.

"Well, that's what happens when you're too close to a boiling pot, Avrel," Carlene pointed out. "I thought the heat would have died down by now, but..."

A harsh wail rang through the air. Everyone in Layden's froze, not daring to move. The wail died away only to be replaced by another, a warning more terrible than the drums.

"What is that?" Frankie whispered. Her fingers gripped the pan she was holding so tightly they were almost white.

"It's a siren." Carlene's eyes were wide, but she kept her voice level and calm. "You know what happens when one goes off, don't you?"

All three girls shook their heads.

"We either get into a building or stay in the one we're in until the bell sounds. That means it's safe to move again."

"But what's happened?" Sami's voice was trembling. "Why did the siren go off?"

"I don't know, and we'll probably never find out." Carlene's eyes strayed towards the café door. Outside, people were racing down the street and into other buildings and shops. No sooner had one person closed a door than it was wrenched open by someone else. The entire street was empty in moments and the siren still went on.

When it died, silence settled on Redcross like snow. Everyone in Layden's kept completely still.

"How long do we wait?" Sami whispered.

"A while. I don't know. It depends on what's happened." Carlene took off her apron and hung it up. "We could be here for hours, girls, and I don't think they're going to bother with the drums."

"Are you saying we might be here all night?" cried Avrel.

"Yes. There is one positive thing: if we do have to stay the night here, we don't have to open first thing in the morning. We could open just before lunchtime and nobody would complain at all." She walked over to the door and locked it; the click seemed to echo around the café.

"Should we get the plates out?" Frankie asked.

"There's no need for that yet. We don't have to eat early because there are no drums to worry about." Carlene smiled brightly as if she'd suddenly thought of something. "Let's sit in the Blue Suite for a bit until it is time to eat. I'd invite you all upstairs to my flat, but the truth is I don't really have one. It's just a room with a wardrobe and a bed - and the Blue Suite's probably nicer."

The Blue Suite in Layden's wasn't as pretty as the one

144

in the Complex, but it was just as welcoming. The walls were painted the colour of a sea on a summer's day, and the floor was littered with plump navy cushions surrounding a single, faded chair. All three girls sat down on the cushions.

"Should we call our families?" asked Avrel.

"You could; they might not be home. And anyway, *they* know where *you* are."

Carlene put her hands on her hips and smiled at the girls. "Since you're my guests tonight, I'm in charge of supper and clearing up as well. There's to be no arguing about this." She spun around and left the Suite, closing the door behind her.

"Does anyone think we should be worried about this?" Frankie asked.

"We should, but Carlene isn't and that makes me feel safe." Sami released her hair from its ponytail and began to twirl a strand around her finger. "I hope we get another message from Milly soon. It's such a relief to know they're treating her well."

"She wouldn't say anything if they weren't," Avrel pointed out.

Sami's finger paused in mid-air. "Now I *am* worried."

There was no clock in the Blue Suite, so the girls simply sat and talked. There was nothing else to do until Carlene came in carrying a tray of food left over from the day's work. The four of them knelt on the floor and ate without spilling anything on the cushions or the carpet.

"How's Leo?" Frankie asked around a mouthful of bread.

Avrel shrugged. "He's all right. This is probably going to be a normal evening for him, siren or not."

Sami's eyes flickered towards Avrel for one quick moment before turning her concentration back to her food.

"Sami, I know about the kiss."

Frankie choked. The bread caught in her throat and she started coughing harshly. Avrel passed her a full glass of water before Frankie could reach for her own empty one. She downed the water, exhaled loudly and said: "Thanks, Avrel. What kiss?"

"It was just one," Sami argued, "and the library door

was closed. It hasn't happened again."

Frankie glanced at Avrel and saw she was smiling in pure satisfaction. "Wait, did you *plan* that?" Frankie cried. She'd always thought she was the sneaky one out of the four friends.

Somehow that wasn't such a good thing to admit now.

"I didn't! I knew Leo liked you, Sami. He's liked you for two years, but I never thought it would go any further. You're always so, so..." Avrel frowned thoughtfully. "I think 'sedate' is the word. And you don't really show how you feel."

"Well, Leo knows now," was Sami's reply.

"Yeah, I guess he does. Carlene, what's the time now?"

Carlene got up and left the Blue Suite. A few seconds later, she was back. "It's half past seven."

Avrel groaned. "It feels later than that!"

If the rest of the night was going to pass like the last few hours, it was going to go by very slowly indeed.

"I know. In a while, I'll bring down some spare blankets; are you all right with sleeping on the floor?" Carlene asked worriedly.

"I don't think I'm going to be able to sleep," Frankie admitted. "I feel so alive."

Something reckless and daring stirred inside her. She got to her feet, not wanting to think about what she was planning to do and allowing it to fill her mind at the same time.

"What are you doing?" Avrel demanded. "Where are you going?"

"I want to try it. Just once."

"Try what...oh no." Sami stood up as well, her face a picture of dread. "Frankie, no. Don't."

"Remember what Carlene said? Oh, sorry, Carlene - you only told *me*. If we're going to get Debra out at night, it's going to be hard to see the map. If we know the way and we have the map, it's going to be even better." Frankie's voice was confident. She had no way of knowing her eyes were soft and pleading. "And there won't be any Watchmen around; they'll be concentrating on...whatever this is."

"What if they aren't?" Carlene asked, folding her arms.

Frankie hesitated. "Well, I'll just hope they are."

146

Carlene sighed. "If you're not back in three hours, I'm locking the door. *Be careful.*"

"And if we get caught..." Avrel began.

"We?" Carlene raised her eyebrows.

"...I'm saying it was Frankie's idea."

The street was dimly lit with a single lamp, presumably for the benefit of the Watchmen. Shadows lay everywhere. Golden light peered through the closed curtains of the nearby buildings. Only one shop had lights on downstairs; Frankie edged carefully away from that one. She didn't dare step out into the middle of the street. If they kept in the shadows of the buildings, it would be harder for anyone to spot them.

Frankie was glad she wasn't wearing her jumper.

Listening carefully for any footsteps that didn't belong to her or her friends, she crept along the wall. If she remembered correctly, this was the way she'd come back from investigating the small gate. Going towards the main gate would have been nothing short of stupid.

Every time they were about to turn a corner, Frankie would look around it first to check nobody else was there, terrified she would see a Watchman approaching in the opposite direction. But the streets were always empty.

Gradually, the buildings grew smaller and shabbier until they were moving among the old, empty homes. Frankie didn't look back at her friends, but she knew they were just behind her.

"Are we close?" Sami whispered.

"Yeah, we're close." The gate wasn't far away; if they turned this next corner and then the one after, they would find the wall. It wouldn't be long now, then all they'd have to do is get...

A solitary figure stood in front of the gate.

Frankie flattened herself against the wall, shaking her head wildly at the others. She thumped the back of her head against the wall twice, eyes clenched shut. This wasn't happening! Why did there have to be someone standing there, and why did it have to be *him*?

When she opened them again, wincing at the pain, she saw Avrel and Sami frowning at her.

Nicholas, she mouthed.

What's he doing here? Sami mouthed back.

I don't know, was Frankie's reply. She pressed a finger to her lips. Slowly, she peered around the corner until Nicholas was plainly in her sight without him being able to see her.

They should go back. She knew that. The girls should creep back the way they had come and hope against hope nobody caught them.

Nicholas stayed right where he was, eyes fixed on the gate.

There was the sound of a latch opening.

Frankie held her breath. She watched as the gate opened and someone stepped through.

"Evening, Nicholas," a female voice said.

"Evening, Ros," Nicholas replied. He was smiling; Frankie could hear it in his voice. "Sorry I couldn't arrange for a better meeting place."

"It's fine. How are things?"

Nicholas moved his shoulders in a lazy, nonchalant way. "Great."

"You're certain he trusts you?"

"Yeah. I don't think he suspects anything."

Frankie swallowed, trying to keep her breathing slow and quiet. Her palms were growing cold and clammy against the wall behind her. She felt Sami take hold of her wrist and squeeze it.

Frankie turned to meet the other girl's eyes. Sami mouthed something, but Frankie couldn't see it properly in the darkness.

"Barton thinks the red armbands symbolise a possible promotion. If he does think something's up, he's keeping it to himself."

Sami mouthed the words again. This time, Frankie knew what they were.

That's Captain Trevel.

It couldn't be. Captain Trevel was on leave; what was she doing back in Redcross? And what were she and Nicholas *doing*?

"Trust me, if he thought something was going on, you'd know. Are my boys behaving themselves?"

"Perfectly. I've got to say, I'm curious why Barton appointed you head of security when only men get to be Watchmen."

148

"He didn't," was the cool answer. "That was his predecessor."

Frankie looked at her friends. They needed to go before they were seen, but if they did leave they wouldn't hear the discussion that was about to take place.

"Speaking of boys, Rowe's on his way," Nicholas said.

Slowly, very carefully, the girls edged away, their feet making no sound. All three watched the streets in both directions; gradually, the voices behind them faded into the shadows.

Just as they reached the street where Layden's was, they heard someone running. Immediately they froze, not wanting to move or even breathe.

A figure fled past them. A faint tinkling sound echoed in the air; the runner came to an abrupt halt and looked at the ground frantically before giving up and disappearing down the street.

Frankie stared at the windows of the buildings surrounding them, but no lights came on. No curtains moved aside. The street was completely silent.

The door to Layden's was still open. Frankie's fingers trembled as she tried to lock the door. Eventually, the lock clicked. Frankie released a shuddering sigh and leaned against the door.

Carlene was still awake. She sat in the chair in the Blue Suite, a worn book in her hands. Blankets were arranged neatly on the floor, with cushions ready to act as pillows.

"Let me guess," she said. "You're not ready to sleep yet."

"No," Avrel replied wearily.

Chapter 17

The bell rang at the exact moment curfew would have finished.

"You'd all better go home," Carlene said. "It's been a long night; I don't think anyone's going to come in until at least lunchtime."

"What about you?" Sami asked. A yawn attacked her in the middle of her sentence; she brought up a hand to cover her mouth. "And what about *them*?"

"We can talk about that later, Sami. Just get going before your families wonder where you are." Carlene's eyelids looked heavy from tiredness. "If anyone saw you, you're in serious trouble."

"We know," Avrel replied, tying her tangled hair back.

Frankie dragged her feet all the way back to her house. Others who had no choice but to take refuge in the nearest building they could find were silent company on the walk.

She opened the door and called out, "Mum, I'm home."

"There you are, Francesca!" her mother's voice called from the kitchen. "Come through and have a hot drink with us."

Frankie entered the kitchen and stopped dead at the sight of Nicholas Ainsley sitting at the table, casually holding a cup of tea.

"What are *you* doing here?"

"Francesca!" Arabella said sharply. "Since when do you talk to guests like that?"

"Since the guest happens to be me." Nicholas put the cup down on the table and shifted around in his chair to face Frankie. "How was your night? You look exhausted."

It took every bit of self-control Frankie possessed not to clench her fists. She forced a smile and folded her arms across her chest. "I am pretty tired, yeah."

"Oh, you know how girls are, Nicholas," her mother said lightly. "When she and her friends are together, odds are they never stop talking. They probably stayed up all night."

"What are you doing sitting in my mum's kitchen?" Frankie asked Nicholas. "You never visited when we were on the island."

"I invited him in for a friendly chat," Mrs. Jamison replied. "I thought you'd like seeing someone from the place you grew up."

Nicholas' smile grew wider. Frankie glowered at him. She would have been glad to see anyone from the Gull Islands so long as it wasn't him, and he knew it.

"There's still tea in the pot. Go on, sit down while I see if we've got any letters." Mrs. Jamison strolled out of the kitchen, leaving her daughter alone with the head of security. Somehow, Frankie managed to pour herself a small cup of tea and sit down opposite Nicholas.

"How's Jack?" she asked.

Nicholas took a large gulp from his cup. "Gone," he said flatly. "The day after he turned eighteen, he caught the first boat he could off the island. We still don't know where he is."

"Yeah," laughed Frankie. "He said he'd be out of there as soon as he was old enough."

"After all the stuff he got up to after you left, I don't think he'll be missed."

Frankie huffed loudly. "Are you ever going to forgive him for that snake incident?"

Now it was his turn to glare at her. "Incident? He thought it would be funny to release two snakes into a school and they weren't harmless little grass snakes, Francesca. They were poisonous. They could have bitten someone. You're lucky the one you found didn't bite you."

Frankie grimaced. Looking back, that hadn't been one of her smartest moments. "I was fine."

"I didn't know that. Seeing you standing on that chair and reaching out for the snake gave me the biggest fright I've ever had in my life. Did you even know they were deadly?"

"Like I said back then, no. I didn't. And it can't have been the *greatest* scare you ever got." Nicholas' reaction to the incident had been one of the scariest - and most humiliating - moments Frankie could remember. She didn't recall anyone ever being so angry with her, including her own mother.

The look in Nicholas' eyes that day hadn't been anger. It had been fear.

"It was."

She shifted, reluctant to look him in the eye.

"Frankie, please look at me."

She did so.

"I'm not your enemy," he said seriously. "I wasn't on the island and I'm not now."

Maybe he wasn't *her* enemy, but he was certainly Barton's. In earlier days, plotting against a Premier was considered treason. Not to mention as head of security, he was a large obstacle between the girls and Debra's freedom.

"What's wrong? You look worried."

He couldn't know what she was really thinking. "I spent the last eight years thinking you were my enemy. It's hard to stop."

"Do you think you can stop?"

Frankie couldn't answer.

"You haven't had any breakfast, have you, Francesca?" her mother asked as she came back into the room. "Wait there, and I'll make you both some eggs."

"Thanks, Mum."

The moment of reconciliation was gone, and Frankie wished she hadn't missed it.

***

"A Watchman was just here," Carlene said as soon as Frankie walked into Layden's.

Frankie stood stock still. She couldn't breathe.

"It's all right, he wasn't after you, but he could have been. He told me Barton's hosting a lunch soon and he wants as many people in the kitchen as possible. By *as many people*, he meant all three of you."

"Thanks for telling me." For a moment, Frankie wondered if a wolf might pick up their scent from the previous night.

The girls could easily have encountered the Wolf-Lords. Why hadn't Frankie thought of that?

Avrel burst into Layden's, Sami close behind her. "We've got a problem. I overheard two members of the security team talking as I walked here. They're going to start searching houses."

152

Frankie felt her guts shrivel. "If they've got Wolf-Lords with them, Debra's in trouble."

"If Debra's landlady complains about her to the security team and asks them to remove her from the house, they could do just that," Carlene said.

"I've got an idea," Frankie said. "How often is the Blue Suite used?"

"Last night was the first time it's been used in months."

"Could you keep Debra here? There aren't any female Watchmen; how many men go into a Blue Suite?"

"They will if they have to," Carlene warned. "What I want to know is, what exactly are they searching the houses for?"

"I think I know." Sami stepped forward, holding out a closed fist. "Remember the runner from last night? This is what he dropped."

She opened her palm, revealing a silver ring with a single stone as green as Sami's eyes. Surrounding the green stone were six smaller white ones.

"Wait." Carlene moved closer, her face pale. "That was Ivy's wedding ring."

"Great. You can give it back to her," Avrel said.

"I can't. She's dead. Her whole family died in the illness."

There was silence for one long and horrible moment.

"Why did that runner have Ivy's ring?" Sam asked. "How did he get hold of it?"

"I've got an even bigger question," Frankie said. "Why was he running with Ivy's ring?"

***

"Are you happy here, Milly?"

Milly glanced up from her bowl of soup. "What do you mean?"

"I mean, do you like it here with us?" Alasdair asked.

Milly looked around her. She was seated at one of the tables in the hall; all around her were people talking, laughing and eating. If not for the wolves, it would have been impossible for her to tell the Wolf-Lords apart from the others. In Redcross, there was a constant sense of movement; nobody was at rest, not even in the evenings or at night.

Kilshiel was completely different. Here, people didn't just hurry through the day. They lived each day.

Milly was allowed to *live*.

She wasn't just sitting around doing nothing in the village. She volunteered for shifts in the kitchen but was only allowed to take one shift every two days. Milly was pleased to find working in the Kilshiel kitchen wasn't much different from cooking in Layden's or the Complex.

Wolves weren't allowed anywhere near the kitchen; this meant any Wolf-Lords had to leave their partners outside until their shift was over, and they weren't allowed to smuggle food out to their wolves. Sorcha had been caught five times trying to do just that.

Milly mostly spent her free time with Alasdair and Sorcha, glad for their company and for the fact that they stayed around her because they wanted to, not because they had to.

"Yes," she said. "I think I am."

Alasdair looked genuinely glad to hear that, but Milly felt a twinge of guilt when she realised her parents and her friends hadn't entered her head much over the past few days. Rachel had said goodbye and told her to send more messages now she was safely at Kilshiel.

Milly would do that as soon as lunch was over.

"When I first got here," she said, "Tamira said Kendrick couldn't afford for me to make a mess of things. What did she mean? I haven't thought to ask anyone yet."

"She shouldn't have told you that. It's not fair on you." Conall whined and Alasdair reached down to fondle his ears.

"What isn't fair on me?"

Reluctantly, Alasdair said: "Gabrielle was supposed to name someone who would take over as leader if anything happened to her. She didn't, and we didn't know until after she died. It was chaos. Kendrick was voted the new *teaghlach* leader but not by much. The deal was he would be allowed to stay leader if he could prove he was good at it. If he doesn't, he'll be replaced. You're the best way of proving to everyone that he *is* a good leader."

"Is this why you asked if I was happy here?"

"No," Alasdair replied firmly. "That was about you, not

154

him. But if they see you *are* happy, maybe they'll go easier on him. Kendrick said you weren't to know because he doesn't want to put pressure on you. Your stay here's supposed to be natural, not an act."

"Is that always how Wolf-Lords prove they're good leaders?" Milly asked. Her insides were slowly turning to ice. "By having someone stay in the village?"

"It's one way, yeah. There are others, but that's the best way to show people outside the *teaghlach* as well."

Milly thought she understood what he was talking about. If Kendrick couldn't take care of an outsider, how could he take care of his own village?

"Hi!" Sorcha came over with a bowl of steaming soup. "Here's your soup, Milly."

"I didn't want another bowl." Milly's lips were numb. She could barely move them.

"Mind if I have it?"

Milly shook her head.

"Thank you!" Sorcha beamed. She sat next to Milly and eagerly began to eat the hot soup.

Debra said she didn't know what the deal her father made with Weatherhill had been, but she'd been part of an exchange, just like Milly. She'd described herself as a guest who couldn't leave.

Milly wanted to ask Alasdair if Weatherhill had done something similar to what Kendrick had. When she tried to open her mouth, something stopped her. He would ask why she wanted to know, and she didn't want to give away the fact that she knew Debra.

Sorcha's spoon hit the table with a tiny clatter. She put a hand to her stomach, breathing in slowly and deeply.

"Sorcha?" Milly put a hand on her shoulder. "Sorcha, are you all right?"

"I don't know." Sorcha swallowed hard, twice. Her face was pale. "I think I need..." Her breathing became harder and faster. Lyall began to whine and paw urgently at Sorcha's knee.

"I'll get the doctor." Alasdair scrambled to his feet and raced out of the hall.

***

155

A small crowd was outside Nairn's house, which also served as the closest thing Kilshiel had to a doctor's place. Sorcha's parents stood closest to the door, their faces almost as pale as their daughter's had been. Lyall paced in front of the door, uttering growls and whines alternately.

"Will she be all right?" Milly asked, her voice barely louder than a whisper.

"I don't know," Alasdair said helplessly. "It depends on what's wrong."

Eventually the doctor opened the door, ignoring Lyall who rushed right past him. Everyone held their breath as he looked at Sorcha's parents.

Then he nodded.

Relief washed over all the watchers. Sorcha's parents gripped hands and walked inside the house. Nairn didn't follow them inside. Instead, he approached Kendrick, who stood a little way away from Milly and Alasdair.

"My guess is it was mushroom poisoning, but it's too early to tell," he said. "I don't think it was a dangerous one; if it was, she probably wouldn't be here."

"If it was, how did she eat it in the first place?" Kendrick asked. "Sorcha knows all about mushrooms; she wouldn't eat a poisonous one by accident."

Nairn's face was grim. "That's what I'm worried about. There's a good chance this *wasn't* an accident."

Alasdair and Milly looked at each other. Once again, Milly saw her fear reflected in someone else's eyes.

Sorcha hadn't been the target. Milly had.

Chapter 18

There were only three thoughts in Milly's head.

Her presence was proof Kendrick could be a good leader. If anything happened to her, it would reflect badly on him. Someone had poisoned a bowl of soup intended for Milly, and Sorcha had been the one to get hurt.

"We don't know what kind of mushroom it was yet," Alasdair said. Under Kendrick's orders, he'd accompanied her back to the small house where they both sat in front of a fire. Conall lay beside Alasdair's chair, anxious eyes turned to his human. "Either it wasn't actually deadly, or Sorcha didn't eat enough for it to be fatal."

"How is she?" Milly asked tentatively. She pressed herself into the back of her chair.

"Nairn wants to make sure she's recovering properly, so he's going to keep an eye on her for a while. I don't think her parents are going to leave her side once during that time." When Alasdair looked at Milly, she could see firelight glowing in his eyes. "You know this means you're going to get an escort again."

Milly nodded. She knew there was no point in protesting, and she didn't want to anyway. There was no point in complaining, either. "Will you be part of it?"

"Did you think I wouldn't?" Alasdair's eyes warmed for a moment before his smile faded. "Kendrick figured out you were the intended target pretty quickly. He said he's going to assign two other people to you, and someone's going to be in the kitchen with the cooks during their shifts. Someone Kendrick knows he can trust."

"But it could be anybody," Milly protested. "What about the people who were in the kitchen?"

Alasdair shrugged helplessly. "They promise it wasn't them but at least two of them wanted Brochan in charge instead of Kendrick, so they're being watched very carefully."

"Wait - Brochan was the other Wolf-Lord who could have become leader?" She remembered seeing Brochan arguing with Kendrick the day she'd caught the fever - and how sharp his wolf's teeth were.

"Yes. He was closest to Gabrielle and quite a few people thought he should be *teaghlach* leader. I wasn't one of them."

The fire was dying. Alasdair got up and used a poker to stir the flames up again. Milly watched him, reluctant to move or even to do anything. There was something deeply comforting about sitting close to a fire in the evening. The light seemed to dance across the walls and over the watchers.

Alasdair came back to his chair and sat down, fondling the back of Conall's neck as he did so. For a few minutes, he and Milly sat in silence.

"It'll be all right," Alasdair said after a while. "You know that, don't you?"

"I know."

"Kendrick's not going to let anything happen to you - and neither are we."

"I know you won't," Milly said softly.

There was a knock on the door. "Who is it?" Alasdair called.

"It's me. Edan." The door opened and Edan walked in, his wolf beside him. He shivered and rubbed his hands together. "You've got a fire going. That's good." He nodded and smiled at Milly. "Nice to meet you properly, Milly. I'm sorry we didn't speak on the journey."

"It's good to meet you now," Milly said.

"I'm going to be another one of your escorts."

Milly felt a wave of frustration and bitterness that she wasn't allowed to do anything about it herself. She was right back to where she started. She wanted to say she didn't need their protection, but the truth was, she did.

And this was about Kendrick, not her.

"Here's what's going to happen," Edan said. He remained standing, casting an impressive shadow that loomed across the wall. "There's at least one of us in the house with you at all times; the escort sleeps on the floor. When you go outside, at least two of us go with you."

"Edan," Alasdair said, shifting around in his chair, "I don't mind sleeping on the floor, but it's not right for one of us to be in the house with her all the time."

"Why not?"

"Because she's a girl," Alasdair replied. "We aren't."

158

"All right, we'll get Tamira to stay here," Edan countered smoothly. "Maybe if the last one had someone stay with her all the time, she wouldn't have ended up dead."

"What?" Milly cried.

Alasdair glared at Edan. "Did you have to say that?"

"Yes," Edan said flatly. "You both needed to hear it! Take this seriously, Alasdair. I wasn't on the migration, but everybody knows what happened."

Alasdair continued to stare at him angrily for a moment. Then he sighed in resignation. "Milly, when you were on the journey, do you remember seeing a girl without a wolf?"

Milly swallowed hard. She nodded.

"Her name was Debra Cameron. She was a guest like you; she was from Ardlaig and Gabrielle brought her back to Kilshiel four years ago. She was...very unhappy with us, but Gabrielle made the deal and it had to be kept."

"Why was she on the migration in the first place?" Milly asked.

Edan and Alasdair looked at each other. "I don't know," Edan shrugged, "and Gabby didn't tell us. Whatever the plan was, the girl disappeared on the journey. The ones Gabby sent to look for her managed to track her to a river that burst its banks." He shook his head. "They never even found her bag."

"But they didn't find a body either. That doesn't mean she's dead," Milly protested. Her fists were clenched so hard, her nails were almost drawing blood.

Was Debra dead? Had she really drowned?

Her chest was far too tight. She tried to inhale, but only drew in short, sharp gasps. She could vaguely see Alasdair getting up, his mouth working silently, but she heard nothing. The fire became one fierce blur.

Alasdair and Conall were coming towards her. She sprang to her feet, but Alasdair caught her before she could even run for the door. He brought her down to a kneeling position, her back against his chest and his arms safely wrapped around her.

"Breathe, Milly. Breathe. You're going to be all right. *Breathe.*"

***

"Here," Leo said, spreading the map out in front of him. "What do you think?"

"It's beautiful." The map showed Redcross in every small detail; Leo even took care to draw the main gate and the two small side gates. Sami noticed there was no exit at the back of the city. She could pick out Layden's and her own home.

"You might want to stay away from the red bits," Leo told her. Sami studied the map again: some of the routes had been shadowed in dark red. To her relief, the route she, Frankie and Sami took the night of the siren wasn't one of them.

"Thanks," she said. "Leo, this is amazing. Have you shown your tutor the other one?"

"Not yet. Hey, um...have Avrel and Milly fallen out or something?"

Sami looked up from the map, startled by the question. "What? No! Why do you think that?"

"For the past few visits she's talked about herself, she's mentioned Mum and Dad and she's talked about you, Frankie and Carlene but she hasn't mentioned Milly. Not *once*." Leo's eyes watched Sami's face intently. "What's going on?"

"The truth is, Milly's not in Redcross and she won't be back for a while." Sami told Leo everything that happened before Milly left with the Wolf-Lords.

Leo got up from his chair. He walked swiftly over to a bookcase and stared at the titles intently, his eyes roving over the leather spines.

"What are you doing?" Sami asked. There was something about the way Leo was looking at the books.

"Wait a second. I know it's here somewhere."

"What's here?"

Leo came back and sat down, a slim blue book in his hands. It was identical to the one Sami read during her first visit. He opened it at the start and began to turn the pages quickly. "This is about customs and traditions of Wolf-Lords. Some of them died out after the wars but the old ones, the really old ones, are still being upheld."

Sami leaned forward, holding her breath until Leo's fingers stopped moving.

"Here it is. It says sometimes an ordinary person will be taken to live with Wolf-Lords in their village for a certain amount of time..."

"Yes, we know that, it's part of a culture exchange." "No, it isn't. OK, sometimes it is part of an exchange, but the whole idea is to see if the person decides they want to live there permanently."

Sami sat frozen in her chair. "What."

Leo turned another page. "At the end of the stay, the person is given the choice to make their home with the wolves or not. If they say yes, that says something good about the *teaghlach* and its leader."

"How does it do that?"

"If the person actually *wants* to stay..."

Sami didn't let him finish. She stood up. "I have to go. Now."

Leo folded up the drawing and pressed it into her palm. "Take this with you."

Sami gave him a quick kiss on the cheek. "Thank you." She ran out of the library and down the corridor, her feet slapping harshly on the floor. She heard the guard outside the library door call after her but knew he wouldn't stop her. He didn't want to risk leaving Leo alone.

Moira met her halfway to the entrance.

"I need to get back to Layden's. Leo..." Sami unfolded the drawing to show Moira. "...gave me this to take home."

"Are you all right?" Moira asked, a concerned frown on her face.

"I don't feel well."

"You don't *look* well. All right, come with me." Moira strode off down the corridor, Sami close behind.

Once Sami was outside, she ran all the way back to Layden's. It was raining heavily but she didn't care. She burst inside the café, looked around frantically for any customers, and said to her astonished friends: "We need to talk. Now."

Without even waiting to dry off, Sami told the girls and Carlene what Leo told her.

"Milly wasn't part of the deal. She was the reason for the deal."

161

"And they're going to ask her to join them?" Avrel was aghast.

"She wouldn't do that," Frankie protested. "Milly wouldn't join the Wolf-Lords, especially after what Weatherhill did to..." She didn't even have time to say the name before realisation washed over her. "Debra was with the Wolf-Lords. She was with them for two years."

"Oh," Avrel said, sitting down heavily. "Is that what they were going to do with her?"

"Are you sure Milly won't join them, Frankie?" Sami asked, giving voice to the unease blossoming inside her. "She's been talking about wanting to leave Redcross. This is her chance."

"She's still got time to decide," Carlene said firmly. "And Sami, you're lucky there weren't any customers here when you burst in like that. Meanwhile, we've got another problem to deal with." She nodded in the direction of the Blue Suite. "Sami, could you go and talk to her?"

"Of course." Sami walked towards the door, ignoring the way her still-wet hair clung to her back. She opened it to find Debra sitting on the chair, staring moodily at the wall.

"How are you?"

"I feel like I've moved from one prison to another."

"It won't be for long. We'll work something out." Sami smiled reassuringly and left the Suite.

Chapter 19

Milly lay curled up under the bedcover, staring at the black wall of her bedroom. Alasdair's words kept whirling around in her mind and heart, even though she'd calmed down a good few hours ago.

If Debra was dead, it was Milly's fault.

She'd made the offer to go with them. She had instigated everything, and she'd got the girls to help Debra escape.

Another part of her mind was telling her there was a good chance Debra was alive. The escape happened after the storm, and Debra wouldn't have been stupid enough to try and cross a burst river.

You jumped into a river, a tiny voice inside her whispered.

Milly shivered. If Debra were desperate enough, she would probably try anything.

No. Milly wouldn't give up hope. She wouldn't.

Tamira was asleep in the next room, wrapped in three blankets. Although there was someone in the house with her, Milly felt completely alone. It had been a while since she'd sent messages to her parents and friends; she wanted to tell the girls what she'd learned but she was terrified someone else might read her message.

What was she going to do?

If Debra was in the same situation two years ago that Milly was now, her disappearance would have had a serious effect on Weatherhill's status as a leader. All Alasdair said about her death was that she'd *fallen.*

Milly clenched her fists under the covers. No. This wouldn't break her. She refused to let thoughts like this affect her, nor would she let the situation she was in right now destroy her.

She was not prey, even if the hunter was human.

***

"Didn't sleep well, did you?" Tamira asked as soon as Milly emerged from her bedroom.

Milly knew there was no point denying it. "Not really."

"I didn't think so. I wouldn't, if I were you." Tamira pointed towards a metal tub filled with water, close to a brightly burning fire. "Go on; I'll give you some privacy."

"Thank you."

"Edan got the water; I just heated it up for you. Kendrick wants to make an announcement before breakfast, so don't be too long." Tamira walked into the bedroom and shut the door firmly.

Milly undressed and stepped into the tub. She scrubbed herself busily, leaving her skin slightly red but soft and clean, and got out of the tub, shivering slightly once the heat of the water was gone.

There was no chance of her being on any kitchen shifts today. She tried not to feel upset about that. If Kendrick told her to stay at home all day until the culprit was found, then she'd do it without questioning him and...

Home.

Milly froze in disbelief, one hand holding a towel around herself and the other reaching out for her clothes. This place felt like *home*. The sound of crackling flame and the smell of smoke was more comforting than her bedroom in Redcross had ever been.

"Are you ready?" Tamira's voice made her jump. "Kendrick wants everyone to be there."

Milly quickly got dressed. "Yes, I'm ready!" she called.

Alasdair, Conall and Edan were waiting outside. When Tamira and Milly emerged from the house, all five set off towards the hall. A sharp wind blew Milly's hair back, tangling it and whipping at her neck. Conall's fur rippled under its hand.

Wolf-Lords, wolves and villagers gathered in front of the hall. Kendrick and Aela stood before the main doors. Kendrick's arms were folded as he stared unflinchingly at the crowd in front of him. He looked as formidable as a gathering storm.

The small group stopped a little to the right of the main crowd. Milly spotted Sorcha's parents; both looked exhausted, tense and restless.

When it was clear everybody in Kilshiel was present, Kendrick spoke. "If anyone knows anything at all about the poisoning that occurred yesterday, now is the time to speak up."

The Wolf-Lords and villagers looked around at each other, meeting the eyes of family, friends, people they'd known all their lives. Then they were reluctant to look at anyone. Some stared in Kenrick's direction without meeting his eyes; others turned their gaze to their feet or the ground.

"Very well," Kendrick said. "Now I'm addressing the poisoner. You've got three days to come forward and confess; if you don't, you will be expelled when we find out who you are."

Milly heard Alasdair breathe in sharply. Several of the Wolf-Lords tensed, and Brochan stared at Kendrick as if he'd never seen him before. Some faces in the crowd looked shocked, while others wore expressions of grim satisfaction.

"If you're innocent, you've got nothing to worry about." Kendrick's gaze travelled from one end of the crowd to the other. "And to the culprit...consider that your last warning."

Aela let out a single, threatening growl.

Kendrick turned around and strode into the hall, Aela beside him. After a few moments, people started to trickle in after him. Edan put a hand on Milly's shoulder and gently pushed her forward.

They made her sit at a table that had been placed in the far corner. They had a perfect view of the rest of the hall, but the cheerful atmosphere that was normally present at mealtimes had disappeared. Conversation was quiet and subdued. Anxious eyes darted from one table to another; Milly barely suppressed a shiver when those eyes ghosted over her.

"Don't worry," Edan said reassuringly. "Your food's being prepared specially, with supervision and taste testing."

"I don't think that'll stop them. Whoever it is doesn't care about using me against Kendrick, so they..." Milly's voice trailed away. The poisoner hadn't intended to hurt Sorcha; if there was a risk of hurting anyone they cared about or anyone in Kilshiel who wasn't Milly, they wouldn't take it.

"Is he really going to do it?" Tamira asked, glancing

from Edan to Alasdair. "Throw the culprit out of Kilshiel? Out of the *teaghlach*?"

"I think he is," replied Alasdair. "Kendrick never lies - and he doesn't bluff, either." Addressing Milly, he said: "It's one thing to leave here voluntarily. To be thrown out or asked to leave is a serious punishment, especially for a Wolf-Lord."

"Even worse," Edan added grimly, "if it is one of us, Kendrick will send a message to the other *teaghlach* leaders telling them who was exiled, what they look like and why. He's basically sentencing them and their wolf to a life of loneliness."

Milly's worried gaze swung to where Kendrick sat. If this was his first serious test of leadership, he was certainly making sure his opponents knew where they stood.

She looked down at her bowl. The porridge looked as heavy as stone, and about as cold.

***

Frankie didn't think she'd ever worked this hard in a kitchen before. There was no time for conversation or playful banter, not even with Joyce, who enjoyed talking to the other kitchen workers. Frankie and the girls prepared lamb with spices rubbed into the meat, peeled and chopped vegetables and washed up as they went along, until Joyce told them firmly to concentrate on the food.

Joyce herself was busy with a pudding that involved apples, crystallised fruit from Anvador, and a thin pastry she made herself. Just the thought of it made Frankie's mouth water, but she knew better than to ask if there would be any left over. If it was as good as she thought it was, there wouldn't be anything left of it.

There was bound to be something to eat at Layden's.

"Well done," Joyce said eventually, causing a loud sigh of relief to echo all around the kitchen. "I am so glad that's over!" She laughed.

"You're not the only one," Avrel muttered.

"It's not over yet," Kaleb said, pointing at the mountain of pans and utensils beside the sink.

An hour later, the three girls emerged from the kitchen.

"I'm so tired, I don't think I'll be able to cook anything else today," said Sami.

"Tell that to Carlene," Avrel snorted. "It's...what are we doing?" She stopped walking. "We've gone out the wrong way."

They had walked right into the main part of the Complex when they should have gone out the back, like they were supposed to. They stood on a small landing with a balustrade, and brown doors scattered along the wall.

"Let's go out the right way before someone asks us what we're...What's *he* doing here?"

Jason Rowe was walking along the opposite landing.

"I know his brother is a Watchman, but Jason wouldn't come here just to say hello to him, would he?" whispered Sami.

"No, he wouldn't." Frankie remembered Nicholas saying Rowe was coming to join them, but not saying which Rowe.

Jason entered one of the rooms on the landing and shut the door behind him.

"Sami, have you still got that ring?"

Sami reached inside the pocket of her jeans and took out the ring.

"You guys wait in that room; if I can't get Jason to come with me, I'll let you know." Frankie hurried down the landing, slipped through the open door and ran towards the one that led to the other landing, paying no attention to the empty red and gold banquet hall she passed through.

Once she was certain she'd found the right room, she waited, hoping against hope Jason would emerge by himself. She wasn't sure how many minutes passed, but eventually he stepped outside.

He flinched when he saw her. "What are you doing here? Get going, they can't see me talking to you."

She put out a hand, blocking Jason's path. "Jason, please, we need to talk," she said. "Now."

"You're not going to give up, are you?"

Frankie shook her head. "No." She took her other hand out of her pocket and, just like Sami had done, opened it up to reveal the ring in her palm.

"What are you..." Jason looked around wildly. "Put that away!"

167

She did so. "Follow me."

As they walked across the landing, she hoped desperately they wouldn't run into Nicholas coming the other way.

"Just in here." She opened the door.

As soon as Jason saw Sami and Avrel, he groaned and closed his eyes. "Tony's going to *kill* me."

"You said your brother didn't know what you were doing," Frankie said. "How'd he find out?" She was more worried about what Nicholas would do if he ever found out about this.

"I wasn't lying when I said he'd arrest me himself. He did. I ran around a corner and came face-to-face with him. I've never seen him more angry or disappointed. At the Complex, Trevel made me an offer: help with the investigation in exchange for a reduced sentence. Actually, it wasn't like that at all. She *told* me I was going to help."

"What investigation?" asked Avrel, folding her arms. "Remember when you arrived, and you got to choose clothes that belonged to people who died from the illness? Turns out that's not all they left behind. You know Carlene wears two wedding rings, right? It's not just to remember her husband; that ring legally belongs to her. A lot of the people who died had family in other places, family who should have inherited a lot of jewellery, heirlooms and other things. Thanks to Barton, that hasn't happened."

"He's using the runners as smugglers," Frankie breathed. "*That's* why he didn't do anything about them before!"

"If he was selling the things nobody's going to claim, that would be fine. But since he isn't selling them, and he hasn't told anyone what he's doing..." Jason let the sentence trail off before asking: "Do you know why the curfew was set in the first place?"

"Because Barton said there were a lot of burglaries?" Frankie asked.

"Yes. Trevel hadn't heard anything about them and since she's head of security, she was the first person who should have known they were happening. She should have been giving the reports to Barton instead of him giving them to her. She figured out Barton was behind the 'burglaries' pretty quickly but didn't have any proof. Thing

168

is, Trevel got a feeling Barton was getting suspicious of her."

"Which is why she left," Sami remarked, "and brought in Nicholas Ainsley. What about the Wolf-Lords?"

"Barton was getting a lot of complaints about runners. He's many things, but he's not stupid." Jason snorted. "Or at least he thinks he isn't. When that Andras guy sent the message, Tony *suggested* the Watchmen use the Wolf-Lords to hunt down runners. Barton didn't know anything about the other messages being sent from Redcross."

"I'm guessing he's warned the runners he's using to stay off the streets?" asked Avrel.

"Exactly." Jason sighed heavily. "Avrel, I am really, really sorry about Leo."

"You suspected he was part of it, didn't you?" "No. He was never supposed to get caught. The route he was on should have been empty; I didn't know Tony had changed the schedule." He shook his head, hair flopping into his eyes. "The only other person Leo knew about was me. I never, ever thought for a minute that he *wouldn't* give me up."

Avrel hesitated, lips poised to speak. Then her mouth closed and she nodded slowly. "It's all right."

"Is it?"

"Yes. I'm not just saying that."

"The Wolf-Lords are going to be here as long as the investigation's going on, aren't they?" asked Frankie.

"Yeah."

Frankie didn't need to look at her friends' faces to know the implications of that were sinking in. As soon as Trevel's investigation was over, there was no need for the Wolf-Lords to stay in Redcross.

Jason's eyes darted from one girl's face to another. "What's going on?" A light came into his eyes. "Does this have anything to do with why you wanted to see me in the first place?"

"The thing is, Jason," Sami said slowly, "we needed to do a little smuggling ourselves. Now we might not have to."

Jason looked at her, a strange smile on his face. "Tony thought you might be a runner, you know. When he got back to the Complex, the first thing he did was ask me about you. I told him you weren't one of us, but he already knew about Avrel being Leo's sister and I had to promise you and the others weren't running. That's why Nicholas threatened me when he saw me talking to Frankie. I gave Tony my word that none of you are caught up in this but whatever smuggling you want to do, you need to know Barton's going to have the security team search businesses next."

"What?" Avrel cried. "When?"

"Seven days. It's part of his 'plan' to track down runners who don't work for him. Tony told Trevel about it, and Trevel's going to make her move as soon as Nicholas and I can get close enough to a Barton runner."

Frankie's mind was racing. If Trevel was meeting Nicholas and Tony - if Jason's words confirmed that Tony was the Rowe brother Nicholas had meant - that meant there was a good chance the side gates weren't being monitored.

Jason's words implied Trevel's move wouldn't be far away, but Frankie wasn't sure if they could afford to wait.

Chapter 20

"I looked at some maps with Leo," Sami said quietly as she entered Layden's kitchen after her weekly visitation.

Frankie scrunched up her face in confusion. "Why did you do that?"

"Because we don't know where the nearest town or city to Redcross is," was Sami's reply, "and Debra's going to need somewhere to go."

"What if that's where she came from the last time?" asked Avrel.

"I thought of that," Sami said, grinning, "which is why I looked up the closest places in the other directions. She probably already knows about them, but I thought it wouldn't do any harm."

"Carlene's been amazing." Frankie held up a small, round biscuit. "She gave me the recipe for some travel flatbreads and some other things Debra could take with her. She can't take much because the knapsack's not all that big."

"Knapsack?"

"Carlene found one in her old wardrobe. It's worn, but it still looks good." Avrel didn't say who the knapsack had belonged to.

Sami's eyes went to the stove. "Watch those potatoes, the water's boiling over."

Avrel quickly rescued them. "Does this mean we're going to go with Debra when she runs?"

"If we are, we'd better hope someone doesn't look out of the window and see us," remarked Frankie.

Avrel scoffed loudly. "What's there to see at one in the morning?"

"Runners," Sami pointed out.

"Oh. Yeah. If Barton's cracking down on runners, there might be more Watchmen and Wolf-Lords out there."

Frankie leaned against the worktop, a troubled expression on her face. "Girls, are we doing the right thing?"

The entire kitchen seemed to go still.

"It's a little late to ask that now!" said Avrel.

171

"Maybe it isn't. What we're doing...we're planning to break the law. We've *broken* the law. If we don't get away with it, we'll have to live with the consequences and if we do, we'll have to live with ourselves. I was up all last night thinking about this; my mind wouldn't let me sleep."

Sami knew Frankie was right. She had no idea which of the two outcomes was worse. Avrel and Leo's parents already had one child in the facility - having both would be unbearable. Sami's parents would be so disappointed in her and from what Frankie implied - or rather, didn't imply - she and her mother did not have the best relationship. This would only make things worse.

But a guilty conscience might be even harder to bear.

Then Sami realised the person whose opinion mattered most in this situation was the only person they hadn't consulted.

"I have an idea," she said. "Why don't we ask *Debra* what *she* thinks?"

Frankie glanced towards the main part of the café. "There aren't any customers."

Sami nodded and headed towards the Blue Suite, forcing down the rising tide of nerves inside her. She knocked on the door twice and pushed it open. Her chest felt strangely light.

Debra sat in the single chair as if it were a throne.

"We've been getting things ready," said Sami, "but we're not sure if this is the right thing to do."

"What? Why not?"

"The Wolf-Lords might be leaving soon." The words 'and because going out after curfew is illegal' threatened to burst out of Sami's mouth, but she kept them contained as she had a feeling Debra would want to know why that was a problem. "What do you think? Do you want to take the risk or wait for them to go?"

Sami didn't want Debra to go back to the Wolf-Lords. She truly, truly didn't.

Debra held her head up, her eyes focused on something Sami couldn't see. "I remember when I first met Weatherhill. I came downstairs and saw her, and I'll never forget the way she just *looked* at me. It was as if she was measuring me up in some way and she didn't like what she saw. I had to live with that for two years."

"No wonder you hated staying with them."

"I hated it more than I can say. My father said I should be proud, that it used to be an honour to live with the Wolf-Lords."

Sami nodded in understanding. For one wild moment, she wondered if her own family would have made a similar deal to the one Debra's father made. Her grandmother died before she could watch the Morels finish sinking into obscurity, but she was obsessed with doing what was best for the family - and the family name. If she thought sending her granddaughter to stay with the Wolf-Lords was a good way of restoring the family name, she wouldn't hesitate to do so.

Debra looked Sami in the eye. "I want to take the chance."

"All right. If you've got any clothes of your own, fold them small enough to fit in a..." Sami stopped talking. Debra most likely knew all about packing clothes in a knapsack. "We'll give you the bag when it's time."

"What about a map?"

"We can get you through the city but once you're outside, you're on your own." Sami handed Debra a small piece of paper. "Do you know how to get to those places?"

Debra unfolded the paper, read it quickly and nodded. "I think so."

"Good. We'll bring you some supper soon." Sami smiled and left the Blue Suite. She was halfway through the main part of the café before the reality of the situation hit her. She grabbed the nearest chair and forced herself to take several deep breaths to calm down.

If her grandmother could see her now, she wouldn't even recognise her.

A customer opened the door. Sami straightened up and put a welcoming smile on her face. "Welcome to Layden's! Would you like a table?"

***

"You've been really quiet," Milly tentatively said to Alasdair. "What are you thinking about?" It was a tactic her mother liked to use whenever Milly or her sisters weren't being particularly social or talkative.

173

"You've been quiet too," Alasdair pointed out.

That was fair enough.

"How did the poison get in the soup in the first place? One of the cooks had to have seen something; nobody else knew you were meant to have that bowl."

"Sorcha did."

The words flew out of Milly's mouth. As soon as she spoke them, she wished she could take them back, but it was too late. They hung in the air, light as a noose.

"What do you mean?" The tone of Alasdair's voice suggested he knew exactly what she meant.

Milly swallowed. "She knows all about mushrooms. She would have known the right amount to eat if she wanted to stay alive. And we've only got her word for..."

"Go on." Alasdair was speaking far too quietly. "There's only her word for it that the bowl was meant for me."

At once, she knew she shouldn't have spoken her thoughts aloud. Alasdair's eyes looked like shards of golden ice.

"I'm sorry," she whispered.

"You should be," Alasdair snapped. "How dare you? Sorcha's..." He shook his head and got up from his chair. "How could you say that about her? You don't know her! If you did, you'd know she would never do anything like that."

He stormed towards the door, Conall at his heels.

"Wait. Wait, I'm..."

The door slammed. Milly was alone in the silent house.

Alasdair was right. Milly didn't know Sorcha. But when Milly looked back over the time spent with the Wolf-Lords, she found herself unable to imagine Sorcha trying to hurt anyone.

The sound of the door opening made her draw in a hopeful breath, and then release it when she saw it was Tamira.

"Everything all right?" she asked, closing the door with a soft click.

Milly nodded. Two tears spilled down her cheeks. "I said something I shouldn't have."

Tamira sat in the chair Alasdair had left earlier. "He'll be fine. He never stays angry for long, not like some others around here."

She reached into her pocket and pulled something out. "I thought you might need this."

Milly held the object in the palm of her hand. It was a tiny knife. The blade glinted in the firelight. Milly turned it back and forth, unable to take her eyes off it.

"Thank you."

"It's just in case you get in trouble and we're not there to help. The poisoner might get a surprise - they won't expect you to be armed."

Milly kept a tight hold on the knife handle for the rest of the evening.

***

"What do we do?" Avrel asked. "You told Debra we'd go with her; does that mean we sneak out of our homes after the drums?"

"I don't know." Sami glanced anxiously out of the window at the grey sky. "I didn't think of that."

Frankie hadn't either.

Somehow, the girls knew without discussing it that tonight was going to be the night. All of them had even put on dark clothes that morning. As the day drew on they found themselves becoming more and more nervous.

Carlene noticed, but said nothing other than a warning to be careful with the plates and glasses. Frankie wasn't sure how she managed to get through the day without dropping at least one of those things. Every so often, she would look down at her hands and see they were trembling.

All the same, she couldn't help feeling a strange excitement. It tingled in her blood and made her stomach churn; it reminded her of playing scaredy-cats on the island with Jack - except if they were caught, the consequences would be much more serious.

Was this how Jason and the other runners felt? If it was, Frankie understood why they kept breaking curfew. The feeling was becoming exhilarating. It made her want to burst out of Layden's and run as fast as she could in any direction.

A hand landed on her shoulders. She jumped, half-expecting it to be Nicholas.

It was Carlene. "Calm down," she said slowly but firmly. "Take deep breaths."

Frankie closed her eyes and did as she was told. She counted backwards from twenty, concentrating on the numbers and not on her heartbeat.

"Is that better?" Carlene asked.

"No." Frankie opened her eyes. "My heart's still racing."

"So is mine," Avrel said. "I feel like I'm about to be sick at any moment."

"Well, one way or another, it'll be over soon," said Carlene. "The food we packed will last about as long as it'll take her to get to the next town, wherever that is."

"But what's she going to do then?" asked Sami worriedly. "She'll have nothing, nothing at..." A tiny frown appeared on her pale face. "Carlene?"

Frankie looked at the expression on Carlene's face and a sickening realisation set in. "Oh, you *didn't.*"

"Just about enough for a few days' food and some rent if she can find it."

"Why would you do that?" Frankie couldn't believe it. "I understand us giving her money if we had any, but *you*?"

"I wasn't doing it for her," Carlene said flatly. "The fact is, you girls and Milly are the closest thing I have to a family and that's the kind of thing family does for each other. Anyway, it was obvious none of you had thought of money."

Frankie didn't know what to say, so she said nothing. One of Carlene's hands was still on her shoulders; Frankie placed one of her own hands on top of it and squeezed.

"I don't know how we can repay you for this," Sami whispered. "Any of this."

"Just don't end up like Jason. Promise me this run will be your last."

"We promise." Frankie spoke for all three of them.

The wail of a siren rose through the air. Outside, there was the sound of people scrambling for safety yet just as before, nobody in Layden's moved.

"That's two sirens in ten days," Avrel said. "That can't be a coincidence."

"I don't think it is either, Avrel, but this is your

chance."

Frankie wasn't quite sure how she and her friends managed to eat the food left over from supper, but before she knew it the plates were empty. Sami spread Leo's map on a different table and they tried to figure out the route they had previously taken.

"This is happening," Frankie breathed. "This is actually happening."

"You knew we were going to do this," Avrel told her. "I know, it's just...Now it's here, it doesn't seem *real*."

"It is real." Sami sounded as if she was trying to convince herself more than Frankie. "Avrel, take off your scarf."

"Why?"

"It's yellow. That's noticeable, even when it's dark."

Darkness fell early because of the clouds overhead. Frankie and the girls waited until it was half past eleven before daring to go and knock on the Blue Suite.

"Ready?" Frankie asked, peering into the room.

Debra shouldered the black knapsack. "Yes."

Beside the chair lay a plate of untouched food.

"You should eat something." Frankie could hardly recognise her own voice. It almost sounded like her mother's. "You're going to be walking a lot tomorrow, and..."

"I don't want anything." Debra pushed past her and walked into Layden's seating area, which was partially hidden in shadows. Sami and Avrel stood by the door, with Carlene positioned closer to the kitchen.

"I'll leave the door unlocked," Carlene said. "Be careful."

Frankie wrapped her arms around Carlene in a quick embrace, which was returned with twice the strength. Avrel hurried forward and switched places with Frankie as soon as the hug was over.

When she stepped back to allow Sami to take her turn, the black-haired girl didn't move. She stood still, amber lamplight falling over her.

"Thank you," Sami said, her voice soft. Carlene looked at her, then nodded twice, her eyes filling with tears.

The street was almost in complete darkness. Keeping close to the buildings, Frankie edged down the street in the direction of the gate. She listened for footsteps but heard none apart for her own and the others'.

She clenched her teeth together to keep them from chattering.

Somehow, the old houses seemed darker and more menacing than before. Frankie's breath sounded far too loud. Once they took a wrong turn and had to double back on themselves. Frankie couldn't believe they'd done that. How could they have been so thick? If a Watchman or a Wolf-Lord had been coming that way, they would have...

Where were the Wolf-Lords?

A group of eight extremely dangerous animals and the humans they were bonded to would have been ideal for handling a threatening situation. Unless Barton - or, Frankie suspected, Nicholas - didn't want to put them at risk.

Her foot nudged against something. Frankie's arms wheeled, her hands grabbing at nothing. She barely stopped herself from falling over onto the cold ground.

Someone - she thought it was Avrel - grabbed her elbows and held her steady. Frankie nodded her thanks and stepped over the object that had nearly ruined everything.

Avrel's hands tightened on her arms. Frankie looked down and felt her whole body turn to stone.

She'd nearly tripped over someone. A figure was lying half-hidden in the shadows.

Frankie knelt beside him; Sami did the same on his other side. Frankie touched the man's left temple and froze when her fingers encountered warm, sticky blood. No wonder they hadn't seen him. It was very nearly pitch black, and he was wearing clothing just as dark as theirs.

"Wait, I know him," Avrel whispered.

"We all do," Sami replied. "It's Jason's brother." "He didn't just trip and bang his head, did he?" Frankie swallowed hard. "I don't think he did."

***

"Well," Tamira remarked. "No surprises in anyone's food, so I think this has been a good evening."

Her words coaxed small smiles out of Milly and

178

Alasdair. There had been an uneasy silence between the two of them all day. Milly wanted to speak to Alasdair badly and it wasn't just because of the argument between them yesterday.

She needed to tell the truth about Debra. She knew she did. Why couldn't she bring herself to simply say the words?

It was nearly midnight. This was the longest Milly had ever stayed awake. She sat curled in her usual chair, with Tamira in the other and Alasdair kneeling on the floor. Conall was leaning against Alasdair's side; in the half-light, he almost looked like a large dog seeking attention. Alasdair reached up and scratched between Conall's shoulders.

"Edan'll be here in a moment," Tamira got to her feet. "I need to stretch my legs for a bit."

"I think it's going to start raining," Alasdair said.

"Then it'll be a quick walk." Tamira grinned at him and Milly, walked to the door and stepped into the night.

After she left, the crackle of the fire was the only sound. Milly watched the firelight dance across Conall's fur and Alasdair's hair, and felt nothing but tenderness and a strange awe. She had seen a side of the wolves and the Wolf-Lords she never would have considered possible if she hadn't come back with them. Why did none of the stories ever talk about that?

"Alasdair, I'm sorry for what I said about Sorcha." "It's all right," he said. "I shouldn't have stormed out like that either." He looked up at her. "Milly, she saved your life. She'd never hurt you."

"I know," she replied, echoing his words. "I'd never hurt you either."

Milly tried to say 'I know' for a second time, but her lips wouldn't form the words. Instead she said: "And I'd never hurt you. Or Conall, or anyone here."

Alasdair smiled at her.

"Alasdair, there's something I have to tell you."

The door opened. Edan and his wolf walked inside. "Glad I got here in time!" Edan said, running a hand through his damp hair. "It's just started raining. Ally, Kendrick wants to see you for a few minutes. He's waiting in his house."

Alasdair reluctantly got to his feet. "We'll be back soon, Milly."

Milly kept her eyes on him until the door was closed. She felt as if she was glowing inside, the fear at speaking the truth completely banished. Lost in her thoughts, she didn't realise Edan was approaching until he sat on the arm of her chair with a satisfied grunt. He looked down at her, a teasing grin on his face and his eyebrows nearly touching his hair.

"What?" she asked.

"You like him, don't you?" Edan asked. He wasn't grinning now.

"Yes," Milly admitted. She did like Alasdair. She knew she would always remember this moment, and the way he smiled at her.

"What happened to Weath...to Gabrielle after Debra died?" she asked. She didn't recognise Edan or his wolf from the migration.

"Well, things weren't good. Gabby lost a lot of credibility with Debra's father. He spread the word that she couldn't be trusted, that she couldn't keep her word and was unable to hold a bargain. Gabby also lost a lot of standing with the other *teaghlachs*."

It was what Milly expected to hear.

When she did tell the truth, she was going to keep Frankie, Sami and Avrel out of it.

"We stayed loyal, of course. Then we all went out for some exercise and Gabby lost her footing. She slipped on something - it could have been some mud or wet grass - and she fell and cracked her head open. She didn't suffer at all." Edan shuddered. "I'll never forget the way her eyes stared. After we buried her, Alban hung around her grave for three days and then he was gone. We haven't seen him since."

"I'm sorry."

"Don't be. It was an accident."

"Did the Mayor even care about Debra?" Milly asked bitterly. "She was his *daughter*."

"Yeah, that's what we thought. A lot of us said Gabby shouldn't have bargained with him in the first place. It wasn't even her idea to take Debra, but the Mayor insisted. It wasn't even a good bargain anyway. Debra was aloof and uncaring and...I never said her father was the Mayor."

The air turned to stone.

"Oh, well," Edan said, shrugging. "It doesn't matter."

He grabbed Milly by the hair. She opened her mouth to scream, only for Edan's other hand to cover her mouth.

"Make one sound and I'll snap your neck."

Chapter 21

Tony was completely still. Frankie couldn't tell if he was breathing or not.

"Is he alive?" asked Avrel.

Through the murky darkness, Frankie saw Sami put a hand on Tony's throat. She waited for a moment before saying: "Yes, he's alive. He's just unconscious."

"What if whoever hit him is still here?" Avrel whispered.

The others went still, watching the shadows closely. The moon above them was the only light they had.

"We can't just leave him here." Blood coming from Tony's head was not a good sign. But the blood was warm. Frankie hoped that *was* a good sign.

"What happens if he wakes up and wants to know why we're here?" Frankie heard Debra shifting around restlessly.

Frankie, Avrel and Sami looked at each other.

"You go on," Avrel said. "I'll stay with him."

"Are you sure?" asked Sami.

"Yes. Go back to Carlene's a different way; you don't want to be here when Tony wakes up."

Frankie put a hand on her friend's shoulder, squeezed tightly and got to her feet. Sami's hand lightly brushed Avrel's other shoulder. As they hurried away, Frankie only looked back once. Tony and Avrel were barely visible.

"Where do we go?" Debra whispered.

"That way." Sami led the way down the narrow street, a lot slower this time. Frankie's shoulders were so tense they physically hurt; she couldn't get Avrel's words out of her head. Tony's attacker might still be around. If they had no problem with hitting a Watchman, they wouldn't care about hurting three unarmed women.

By now, they were nearly at the wall. All they had to do was reach the gate, open it and allow Debra to slip through, then go back to Layden's.

What if the attacker returned to Tony and found Avrel there?

Sami stopped walking and threw an arm out to the

side. Frankie nearly collided with Debra's back; she edged around her and saw why Sami was frozen to the spot.

A light glowed around the corner.

Frankie closed her eyes, despairing at her own idiocy. Of course they wouldn't be the only ones to take advantage of the siren. Nicholas probably set both sirens off so that he could meet with Trevel. He was clever enough to do that.

The girls could wait until the meeting was over and hope against hope Nicholas didn't come their way - or that Tony didn't come up behind them with Avrel's arm in his grip.

A *click* echoed in the darkness. Frankie's breath caught in her throat. She'd heard the sound before on the island, but this time it filled her with fear.

It was a gun being cocked.

***

It was becoming harder to breathe. Edan still kept a tight grip on her hair and over her mouth; if Milly stumbled or tripped, he might really break her neck.

Nobody was outside because of the rain. Milly's hair was already sticking to her head. That didn't matter. Nothing mattered except where Edan was taking her and what he was going to do.

Her eyes darted down to where she thought his wolf was, but she couldn't see it in the darkness.

"I'm going to take my hand off your mouth now," Edan said, "but if you even try to scream, you're going to regret it. That's a promise."

A growl sounded somewhere close to Milly's legs.

Milly gasped in a breath as soon as her mouth was free, which turned into a stifled yelp of pain as Edan took hold of her left shoulder. She couldn't even see where they were headed - but if she got the chance to break free, she would take it and run.

Wait. She *did* know where they were going. She could just about see the looming shapes of the three hills.

He was going to drown her in the stream.

The realisation should have terrified Milly, but somehow she felt no fear. All she felt was a calm, chilling resignation mixed with the knowledge that she didn't want to die.

"You poisoned the bowl and told Sorcha to give it to me. What mushroom did you use?"

"That's the beauty of it. I didn't use a mushroom. I chopped up a special type of leaf and put it in Sorcha's *first* bowl. I knew you didn't order a second and Sorcha loves mushroom soup, so she'd happily eat a second bowl if you didn't want it."

"Killing me isn't going to help," Milly pleaded. "You heard what Kendrick said: if you say it was you, he won't banish you. You've still got one day left. This isn't going to help you."

"Yeah, I know it won't." Edan chuckled. "I didn't think that through. Didn't realise Kendrick actually cares about you. Why would he? Gabby thought Debra was just a bargaining tool. If I remove you, I remove Kendrick. It'll be better for the *teaghlach* if Brochan's in charge. They'll see."

"They'll know it was you. They're not stupid." Milly could hear herself becoming more frantic. "Please. Please. You don't have to do this."

"I know." Edan's voice was heavy with regret. Milly remembered the way he hugged his son, and the tender kiss he gave his wife.

The image was replaced with pictures of Milly's own loved ones: her parents, her sisters, her friends, Carlene, Alasdair, Sorcha, Kendrick...

Goodbye.

She blinked back tears and willed her hands to stop shaking. Slowly, she loosened her right fist and moved it, ever so slightly, towards the pocket where she kept Tamira's knife.

***

"I'm going to say this one more time," Barton's voice said calmly. "Get against the wall, now."

Frankie didn't dare move. She heard footsteps, which meant Barton's order was being obeyed, yet her own feet stayed stuck to the ground. Sami took hold of her hand and held it tight.

"How'd you figure it out?" Nicholas asked. He didn't sound as if he particularly cared how Barton knew the truth.

"First of all, I'd like to congratulate you on doing a very impressive job as Rosamund's replacement. In fact, you were so good that I only grew suspicious when I remembered you came from the Gull Islands. I couldn't understand why Rosamund would want someone from there. Anthony Rowe could do just as good a job - maybe even better."

Slowly, carefully, Frankie stepped towards the light. She peered around the corner to see Nicholas and Trevel standing with their backs pressed to the wall, their hands raised just high enough for Barton to see them. Neither of them noticed her. Their eyes were fixed on Barton's face instead of the weapon in his right hand.

Once Frankie saw the black, cold gun, she couldn't take her eyes away from it.

"Did you really believe I was that stupid, Rosamund?" Barton asked. "I have my informants as well."

"You were *stealing*," Trevel spat. "I couldn't let you get away with that. What kind of person would I be if I did?"

Frankie stepped away from the sight. *We've got to do something,* she mouthed. They had to. Nobody else was coming.

Sami nodded. She closed her eyes, took a deep breath and walked into the shadows of the alley.

*What are you **doing**?*

Frankie saw Sami's lips say: *It's all right. Trust me.*

"Unfortunately, I can't let you get away with this." Frankie's head whipped around.

"You can't exactly shoot us," Nicholas said. If he was afraid, he was doing a very good job of concealing it.

"Oh, I didn't shoot you, Nicholas. Anthony did. He suspected you were smuggling jewellery, so he followed you. Unfortunately, he was left with no choice but to use a gun. Sadly, you or Rosamund managed to inflict a rather nasty and *fatal* head wound. Now..." Barton motioned sharply with the gun. "...start walking."

"Where's Tony?" Trevel growled.

"Now."

They were coming towards Frankie and Debra. If they

turned left, they would miss them but if they kept walking...

"Turn here," Barton ordered.

There was a loud clatter from somewhere to the left. The next moment, the air rang with two gunshots.

Frankie ran out of the shadows and hurled herself onto Barton's back. She gripped around his shoulders tightly, holding on with every ounce of strength she had. Her legs kicked wildly as he spun around.

Goodbye.

Frankie loosened her hold in shock. Immediately, Barton slammed her into the edge of the nearest building. Pain shot through Frankie's back and shoulder. She was clutching Barton's jacket with only one hand now.

Barton grunted with pain and staggered to the left. Frankie let go completely, slumping heavily to the ground. She was half-blind with dizziness.

"No, you don't." Nicholas' voice was dark with menace.

Frankie's vision cleared just in time to see him standing over Barton, the gun in both hands. Barton raised his hands quickly.

Frankie slowly stood up. Her back jarred and she winced.

"Are you all right, Frankie?" Nicholas asked without taking his eyes from Barton.

She nodded, and immediately wished she hadn't. "Yes. Thank you."

"Frankie!" Sami came hurrying up, white-faced and shaking. Her clothes and hair were covered with red dust.

Running footsteps grew louder and louder. Avrel and Tony burst onto the scene, Tony holding something pressed to his head. The yellow material was stained with blood. Frankie had barely enough time to wonder why Avrel had even brought her scarf with her when Trevel returned, Debra's rucksack firmly grasped in one hand and Debra's arm in the other.

"Who are you?" Trevel demanded. "What's going on? What are you all doing here?"

***

Milly could hear the stream now. It wasn't far ahead. She

gripped the handle of the knife tightly.

"I want you to know," Edan said, sounding slightly out of breath, "that I've got nothing against you personally. This is about Kendrick, not you. Sorry if that's not much of a consolation."

Milly slashed at his arm with the knife. He yelled with pain and let go of her. She whirled around and ran as fast as she could. Wind and rain hit her face, blinding her.

Behind her came a snarl. Fear made her heart beat faster and gave speed to her legs. Edan's wolf was nearly on her. She could almost feel its teeth snapping at her ankles. She couldn't let go of the knife. She wouldn't. Her breath was as loud as the wind.

Paws landed on her back and she sprawled to the ground. Fangs grasped the arm she held up to protect her face and throat. Milly screamed and instinctively thrust upward with the knife.

Suddenly the air was filled with growls. A furry shape collided with Edan's wolf, sending him rolling over on the ground. Milly's arm was wrenched to the side and she heard her sleeve tear.

She tried to struggle to her feet only for a hand to grab her hair again. Blood dripped down her face as Edan pulled her to her feet. He grabbed her wrist and moved it sharply towards her; Milly let go of the knife and it fell onto the wet grass just as her hand collided with her stomach.

"Edan!"

Edan froze. He pulled Milly to stand in front of him, one hand in her hair and the other closed around her throat.

"Let her go," Kendrick said quietly. Milly couldn't see him, but she knew he was standing in front of them.

Milly heard Edan's wolf growl. A louder one from Aela quickly silenced it.

"Please," Edan begged. "Laird's hurt. She stabbed him." His blood trickled down Milly's cheek and over his hand. His grip on her throat wavered slightly and he immediately tightened it.

"You're both hurt," Kendrick replied, "and when we get back to Kilshiel, we'll treat both of you."

Milly could sense him willing her to keep looking at

him, so she did.

"But you're also surrounded," Kendrick continued. "If you let Milly go now, the consequences won't be so severe. If you don't, or if you hurt her, they will be very severe and we both know you don't want that. You don't want to hurt her, either."

Milly stayed very still. Edan's grip caused her to raise her head and draw in a gasping breath. Her fists were clenched at her side. She was certain Edan did want to hurt her now, because she'd just done something he would consider unforgivable: injure his wolf.

These could be her last moments alive. She knew what she needed to do with them, even as her mind screamed at her not to speak.

"Gabrielle was going to let Debra go, wasn't she? That's why she was on the migration."

Silence was the only answer. Milly swallowed and forced the next five words out of her mouth.

"It's my fault Debra's dead."

Edan tensed. "What are you talking about? No, it isn't. The girl drowned."

"It was my idea. She wouldn't have gone otherwise." Milly looked directly at Kendrick, right where she thought his eyes were. "I am so, so sorry."

She hoped she wouldn't feel the snap.

Edan let go of her. His fingers fell away from her throat and he dropped to his knees. "I...I feel dizzy."

Dark figures ran forward and took hold of him just as someone took hold of Milly's shoulders and eased her away.

It took her a moment to realise it was Sorcha.

Chapter 22

"Let me see your arm."

Nairn took hold of Milly's elbow and pulled it gently away from her side. Her fleece lay discarded on the floor; a large part of the left arm had been ripped away and dangled to the side like a dead leaf.

"Good thing you were wearing that fleece," the doctor said. "It might have saved your arm. The bite isn't as deep as it could have been. I'll clean and bandage it now."

Milly kept her arm as still as she could while Nairn cleaned it. She felt cold and very sleepy, but she knew she couldn't rest.

"What's going to happen to Edan?" she asked. "We're going to decide that soon," was Kendrick's reply. "Something like this hasn't happened in a very long time. This isn't going to be easy for anyone."

Milly knew he was thinking of Edan's wife and son.

"Thank you," she said softly, finally turning to look at him.

"Did those other girls know?"

Milly went very still. She forced herself to keep looking at Kendrick's eyes.

"The girls you were friends with on the journey, the ones you were always talking to - do they know about Debra as well?"

Milly hesitated. Then she nodded.

"Don't you know Edan could have killed you?" Now Kendrick sounded angry.

"I thought he was going to kill me anyway," Milly whispered. "I've been trying to work up the courage to tell someone since I heard she was dead. If I didn't speak then..." She couldn't finish her sentence. "I truly am sorry."

Kendrick's expression was completely unreadable. "Once your arm is bandaged, I want you to go back to the house and stay there until someone comes for you. Tamira's going to keep you company. Don't go *anywhere*. Understand?"

"Yes."

The door to Nairn's house opened and Brochan walked

in. "Trevel's on the phone. She's calling from Redcross."

"I'll be right there." Kendrick gave Milly one last look. "Stay in the house." Then he and Brochan were gone.

"There," Nairn said. "Finished."

Milly thanked him and left, her arm throbbing and twinging. It was strange, but she hadn't even noticed the pain before arriving at the doctor's.

The sun was just starting to emerge from the horizon, casting a pale and cold light in the distance. Milly could just about make out the shape of her house; shivering, she headed for the small building.

When she opened the door, she was met by the tiny glimmer of a lamp. The fire was now a pile of grey, lifeless ash.

Tamira stood in the middle in the room. "Hi," she said. "You OK?"

Milly wanted to say 'yes', but she couldn't. Slowly, she went over to the nearest chair and sank into it, covering her mouth with her hand to stifle the sobs that threatened to burst out.

Tamira walked up to the chair, knelt in front of it and wrapped her arms around Milly's shoulders. Something shattered and Milly broke down, releasing all the dread, exhaustion and fear inside. She collapsed against Tamira's shoulder, weeping in despair.

She was still alive, but she felt as if she had lost everything.

***

Milly opened her eyes to see sun pouring into her bedroom. She sat up slowly. She didn't even remember moving into the bedroom.

Breakfast would be over by now, and the villagers and Wolf-Lords would be getting on with the day. The cooks would be either washing up after breakfast or arriving to get lunch prepared. Perhaps, back in Redcross, Sami, Frankie and Avrel would be frying sausages and eggs for sandwiches or chopping vegetables for soup. Milly's parents would be at work. Perhaps they'd received another message from Susanna - or maybe even one from Rachel.

Milly looked down and saw a large patch of dried blood

on her blue T-shirt.

She peeled off her clothes and folded them in a neat pile. She picked up clean clothes and got dressed without caring to see what she was putting on.

Five minutes later she stepped out of the bedroom, her hair brushed and lying below her shoulders.

"Oh, you're awake." Tamira sat on the chair closest to the empty fireplace. "You look like you need to sleep for the rest of the day. Are you actually going outside in that?"

Milly's fingers brushed against the skirt of her dress. "I'm supposed to stay in the house."

"Until Kendrick says otherwise," Tamira pointed out. "Speaking of Kendrick, Alasdair came here earlier to fetch you; I told him you were still asleep."

Milly's stomach lurched nervously, but she ignored it. "Tamira, thank you so much for giving me that knife. I'm sorry I dropped it last night."

Tamira pulled the knife out of her pocket, tossing it into the air and catching it by the handle. "Alasdair brought it back. But I'm glad it helped. I'm also glad Edan gave up when he did - and not just for your sake."

"Are they badly hurt?" Milly would never forgive herself if Edan or Laird died.

"They'll recover. That's all you need to know," Tamira replied firmly. She folded her arms and regarded Milly through hazel eyes. "I was wrong about you."

"No, you weren't. You saw through me from the start."

"Yes, I did," Tamira said bluntly. "But you can be right and wrong about someone at the same time."

There was a sharp rap on the door. Milly recognised Alasdair's knock. Tamira looked at her, eyebrows raised.

Milly nodded.

"Come in," Tamira called.

Alasdair opened the door. His hair was slightly tousled and his eyes stood out in his pale face. "Kendrick wants to see you."

"I'm coming."

All Milly could do now was face the consequences. If she was lucky, Kendrick would tell her to leave.

It was surprisingly warm outside the house. A breeze blew the dress back against Milly's legs as she walked beside Alasdair, Conall by his other side. Milly let her gaze roam all over Kilshiel, taking in everything she saw.

"How did Kendrick know Edan was the poisoner?" she asked without looking at Alasdair. "Was it when you turned up to see him?"

"No. We just thought there'd been a mix-up or something."

"So how did he know?" Now Milly did look at him.

Alasdair returned her gaze, then looked down at the ground. After a moment he raised his eyes again, staring straight ahead of him. "He didn't. I really don't know how to tell you."

He met her eyes again. Milly couldn't look away from them. She felt him take her hand and she found herself breathing a little easier. She would miss Alasdair deeply, and she didn't want to leave.

Kendrick's house was just ahead of them. Milly straightened her shoulders and held her head up. They were not going to see her cry.

She raised her free hand and knocked. Kendrick opened the door; Milly tried not to step backward when she saw him.

"Thank you, Alasdair," Kendrick said. "Could you leave us for a few minutes?"

"Sure." Alasdair tightened his grip on Milly's hand for one moment, then he was walking away.

"Come in, Milly." Kendrick held the door open, allowing Milly to step inside. She looked at the bare stone walls, the two dark green chairs and the crimson oval-shaped rug on the floor.

"Do you remember Brochan saying there was a call from Redcross this morning?"

"Yes." Milly's throat was dry.

Kendrick looked down at her, his expression serious. "I want you to know what I learned from that call has no influence on what's about to happen now. Do you understand?"

"I do."

Kendrick put his hands on Milly's shoulders and kissed her on the forehead. In his eyes she saw something she had never expected.

It was forgiveness.

Kendrick was smiling at her.

Milly couldn't help it. She broke down in tears again. Kendrick guided her over to one of the chairs and sat her down, handing her a piece of soft material and waiting for her to calm down. Milly wiped her face with the cloth. There was a lightness inside her that hadn't been there before.

She knew she didn't deserve it.

"Debra's alive."

Milly froze, the material close to her cheek. "She's what? Are you sure?"

"Yes. She's in Redcross." Kendrick pulled the other chair over and sat opposite Milly. "There was an incident last night involving your friends. Don't worry, they're all right," he said as Milly's eyes flickered fearfully. "There are some things I need to tell you."

Milly sat up in the chair, the material crumpled in her hands.

"Why do you think we came to Redcross in the first place?"

"We thought it was to help Barton deal with runners," Milly said, confused.

"Before we left, Captain Trevel contacted me and said Barton was using us as a front. He's been stealing jewellery and smuggling it out of the city. Trevel told me to contact her replacement as soon as he arrived, since he'd be handling the investigation. I asked for volunteers to stay in Redcross after you were chosen."

That made sense. There was no reason for Kendrick himself to stay after he got what he wanted.

"Barton realised what was happening and cornered Nicholas and Trevel while they were meeting last night. Your friend Francesca - she's the girl in the red jumper?"

"Yes."

"She distracted Barton and Nicholas managed to get hold of the gun. From what I've been told, Nicholas is proud of her and wants to strangle her at the same time."

"How much trouble are they in?" Milly asked uneasily.

***

"The answer is: a lot."

Sami, Frankie and Avrel sat in the Premier's office,

193

facing Nicholas. He sat behind the desk, Tony Rowe standing at his right side. After a long and very thorough explanation, the girls spent a torturous few hours waiting in a bedroom in the Complex, unable to sleep at all. They were still wearing the clothes from last night. Frankie wanted to call her mother but was unable to find the courage to ask. She didn't even know what to say.

Frankie wondered how Carlene was.

"Thing is," Nicholas said, leaning forward to look at the three girls, "you also saved our lives. If it hadn't been for you, Barton would have got away with smuggling *and* murder."

"Thank you for that, by the way," Tony added sincerely.

"Trevel's left it up to me to decide what to do with you." Nicholas sat back, his fingers linked together. "The two things don't exactly cancel each other out. I can't let you get away with breaking the law, but we owe you our lives."

He glanced at Frankie. It was only for a moment, but she thought she saw his lips twitch into a smile.

"What about Leo and Carlene?" Avrel asked.

Nicholas turned his gaze onto her, serious again. "What *about* Leo and Carlene?"

"Are they going to be in trouble because they helped us?"

"What happens to them isn't your concern," Nicholas said flatly. When Avrel opened her mouth to protest, he added: "I know - he's your brother and you're worried about them both, but right now you've got bigger things to worry about."

"Leo's sentence might be extended," Tony added, "but they haven't decided on that yet."

"What happens now?" Sami's voice was quiet. "Well, Barton's not going to be Premier anymore. That's obvious."

"I'm going to see if I can get Trevel nominated," Tony said. "Don't tell her, though!"

"I'll be very surprised if she doesn't get rid of the curfew the first chance she gets," Nicholas remarked.

Frankie hoped that was the case. It was too bad she and the others probably weren't going to experience that freedom for a long while.

"Nicholas, I'm not going to persuade you to go easy on

194

us. But before you tell us what our punishment is, I want to say we thought we were doing the right thing. We thought we were helping Debra, and I'm not sorry for that." Frankie looked at Sami and Avrel. "At least, *I'm* not."

"Are you aware the Wolf-Lords thought Debra was dead?" Nicholas asked.

"No." Sami sounded completely stunned. "We weren't."

"What happened on the migration needs to be taken into account as well."

Frankie barely stopped herself from groaning.

***

"If you want to go home because of this, I'll arrange an escort for you. Nobody would blame you if you did want to leave."

"Am I still welcome here?" Milly asked.

"Yes."

"Then I'd like to stay."

Kendrick smiled broadly at her. "I'm glad." The smile vanished, and the serious expression returned to his face. "Since you do want to stay, I need to tell you about the final part to the tradition."

Milly was only half-listening. She wondered if Kendrick would have held her responsible if Debra really had drowned - and if she would ever have forgiven herself.

Beside the chair, Aela looked up at Milly with eyes that seemed to see right through her.

"The tradition is a very old one, and it goes back to the days of the first Wolf-Lords. It used to be an honour to be asked to live with us, but the wars changed everything. Several of the old traditions that involved people outside the villages and the *teaghlachs* died out because everyone was terrified of us."

"I know it proves to the *teaghlach* that their leader can be trusted," Milly said. "Is it always part of a deal?"

"Most of the time," admitted Kendrick. "But it also has a third purpose."

Milly nodded, suddenly aware of a flicker of apprehension deep inside her.

"When the six months are over, I'm going to ask you if you want to live here for good."

195

Milly couldn't find her voice. She stared at Kendrick in amazement.

"You'll have the rest of your time here to think about it, and on your last night I'll tell everyone what your decision is."

"If I do stay, would it be a good thing for you and the *teaghlach*?" Milly asked, her voice trembling.

"That doesn't matter," Kendrick replied firmly. "It's got to be what *you* want, and it has to be of your own free will. But whatever you decide, you'll always have a home with us."

***

"You broke curfew, so that's two months. You deliberately went out after a siren twice, which is putting yourself in danger *twice*, so that's another four months for each time." He looked directly at Frankie. "Believe me, if I made the law here, I would double the siren penance."

"Believe me, I'm really glad you *don't* make the law here."

"I'll bet you are. But the fact remains that you helped stop Barton and you saved our lives, so Ros is going to make you a deal. You've got two choices. The first is, you serve two months in the facility: one month for breaking curfew and the other month for the siren. *Both* sirens."

Frankie, Sami and Avrel looked at each other. That was more lenient than they could have imagined.

"What's the second choice?" asked Sami.

"The Wolf-Lords are going home in two days. The second option is this: you go with them and stay in their custody until Emilia's finished her time with them. Once that's over, you'll be escorted back here - or they might give you the same choice they'll give her."

"It's a choice between being locked up or banished?" Avrel cried. "The Wolf-Lords are going to *hate* us."

"Actually, they don't hate you," Nicholas told her. "Ros and I had a little chat with Andras and told him about Debra; he was surprised, but he took it quite well. If he did, I promise the rest of the Wolf-Lords won't be giving you any problems."

Frankie hoped that meant they weren't giving Milly

any problems.

"Speaking of Andras, he says Emilia's been doing well with them. There was an incident last night with someone who doesn't like Andras, but Emilia's fine. She's adapted pretty nicely to a life outside the walls. If you take the second option, maybe you will, too."

Then Frankie understood what Nicholas was saying. Going with the Wolf-Lords was a reward, not a punishment - and they would arrive home around the same time Leo was released from the facility.

"Oh, and don't worry about your friend Debra," Nicholas added casually. "From what I've been told, Carlene's willing to offer her a job at Layden's. And Leo's art teacher says she might be able to take him on as a proper apprentice once he's been released, no matter when that is."

Sami and Avrel couldn't hold back their smiles. "When do we have to decide?" Frankie asked. "The Wolf-Lords leave tomorrow morning with or without you. If you want to go with them, I'll have to know by midday. You've got some time to think about it."

Sami stood up. "Thank you," she said, "on behalf of all of us." She looked at Tony. "Are you going to be lenient with Jason? He *did* help you and Trevel."

"Come on. He's my brother." Tony smiled in the exact way Jason did. "He knows that, no matter what."

The three girls walked towards the office door. Avrel left first, closely followed by Sami. Before she closed the door, Frankie gave Nicholas the first genuine smile she had ever given him and was rewarded with one in return.

Frankie, Sami and Avrel walked side by side through the silent streets. Avrel wouldn't take her eyes off the ground and Frankie knew she was torn. She didn't want to stay in the facility - but if she did, she would be living in the same place as her twin. Sami looked calm but resolved.

As they walked, Frankie mulled over the options in her mind and knew that for her, there was no choice.

Everything was going to be all right, no matter what the others decided. Frankie held her head up and looked straight into the morning.

Milly wandered towards the hills, the sounds of Kilshiel drifting further and further away from her. Above her was a perfect sky; the sun warmed her arms and shoulders and the breeze made her dress blow gently. The hills were a beautiful shade of green; they turned darker every time a cloud passed overhead.

As she raised her eyes, Milly saw the black shadow of an eagle in the sky.

Before long, she reached the stream. The water was as clear as glass; pebbles and stones shone beneath the surface. A rock was close to the edge of the stream. Milly walked over and sat down, carefully gathering her skirt beneath her.

She stayed completely still and watched the water flow past her.

Milly couldn't go back to Redcross. She knew that now. Whatever she did, there was no going back, no matter how much the thought gnawed at her. She could either move on and make a life for herself or accept the life that had been offered to her.

In Redcross, her life felt like a circular pathway that led nowhere and all she'd wanted was the chance to take a different road. Now she had the chance - and she wasn't sure what to do.

"Mind if I join you?"

Milly glanced up to see Sorcha standing beside her. The other girl was slightly thinner than the last time she'd seen her. Lyall stood protectively by Sorcha's side.

"Sure."

Sorcha knelt on the grass beside Milly's rock. "Last time we were both beside running water, things didn't go so well."

Milly laughed. "The stream looks pretty shallow. I don't think we're in any danger."

They sat quietly for a few minutes. Milly was grateful for Sorcha's company but wasn't quite sure how to tell her, so she kept quiet.

"Did you know Aela's pregnant?" Sorcha asked when the silence became a little too uncomfortable.

"Really? That's wonderful!"

"Yup! We're going to have new wolf cubs - and new Wolf-Lords, when the cubs are old enough." Sorcha looked up at Milly. "I know about the choice, Milly. You've got five months to make your decision; you don't have to do it right now."

Milly said nothing. She was thinking of her family and friends. How was she going to tell them about this?

Would she ever see them again?

"I am glad I came here," she said softly.

"I'm glad too!" Sorcha hesitated for a moment. "So is Alasdair. He really likes you, Milly. I'm not trying to pressure you."

"I know."

Milly knew she liked Alasdair as well. But that was just it: like. It could develop into something more, but the question was whether it would and if she would be willing to see if it did.

"Is that why he put my name forward?"

"He didn't."

"What do you mean?" Milly asked.

"Alasdair didn't put your name forward. I did. I saw you weren't scared of Conall and Lyall, and I thought you'd be perfect." Sorcha smiled at Milly. "And you were." She got up and walked away, Lyall close behind her.

Milly stayed on the rock, warming herself in the sun's rays and listening to the song of the water. The eagle continued to circle above her. After a while, Milly stood up and walked back the way she had come.

The village was there, waiting for her.

The End

I hope you enjoyed reading *Wild Rose*! Please consider leaving a review on Amazon or Goodreads. Reviews are a great way to help readers find books they will enjoy.
Thank you!

Acknowledgements

First of all, I want to thank God for everything. Including this. You gave me this talent and I'm using it for Your glory.

Mum and Dad, thank you for your love and support. Thank you for believing in me, and for being willing to read the first drafts!

My writing coaches, Laura, Rowan, Diana and Zulema - thank you so much for your help and guidance. I'd also like to thank Monica Hay, Emma Coquet and the rest of my OneNote writing group. Going on this journey with you has been a privilege.

Alydia Rackham, your fairytale retellings are inspired, original and breathtaking.

K.M. Weiland, thank you so much for your 'Outlining Your Novel Workbook'. I can't tell you how big a help it's been.

Thank you to Andy Clarke, who I first heard sing the ballad that inspired Gabrielle Weatherhill's name - and her backstory.

Thanks to the staff of my favourite coffee shop, who make amazing brunches and chocolate brownies.

And last, but by no means least, thank *you* for reading this.

Coming next...

Dark Rose

204

About the Author

Lucy lives in a seaside town. When she was five, someone gave her a story notepad and she has never stopped writing since. She has loved books ever since she can remember. Eventually, she decided to write a book herself.

https://www.facebook.com/lucywintonroses/

https://twitter.com/winton_lucy

Printed in Great Britain
by Amazon